ZACKTASTIC

TWINSANITY

Courtney Sheinmel

Book Two

PUBLISHED BY SLEEPING BEAR PRESS

Sleeping Bear Press™

2395 South Huron Parkway, Suite 200, Ann Arbor, MI 48104
www.sleepingbearpress.com
© Sleeping Bear Press

Printed and bound in the United States.
10 9 8 7 6 5 4 3 2 1

Library of Congress Cataloging-in-Publication Data

Names: Sheinmel, Courtney, author.
Title: Twinsanity / written by Courtney Sheinmel.
Description: Ann Arbor, MI : Sleeping Bear Press, [2017] | Series: Zacktastic ; book 2
Summary: "Shortly after Zack begins his training at genie school, his twin sister, Quinn, starts experiencing some strange symptoms. It turns out she's a genie, too, and Zack is not happy about it. But when Quinn is kidnapped by evil genie Linx, Zack and his new genie friends must rescue her"—Provided by the publisher.
Identifiers: LCCN 2017002854
ISBN 9781585369362 (hard cover)
ISBN 9781585369379 (paper back)
Subjects: | CYAC: Genies—Fiction. | Wishes—Fiction. |Kidnapping—Fiction. Brothers and sisters—Fiction. | Twins—Fiction.
Classification: LCC PZ7.S54124 Twi 2017 | DDC [Fic]—dc23
LC record available at https://lccn.loc.gov/2017002854

For Lia, Marco, and Bianca

1

A Few Words from Quinn

Every morning before school, my second best friend, Madeline, comes over for breakfast. Together we use Madeline's cell phone to call my first best friend, Bella.

I'd use my own cell phone to call Bella, but I don't have one. Even though I've begged and pleaded with my mom about it. It's the one and only thing my twin brother, Zack, and I agree on. He begs and pleads for one, too.

Not that Zack has any friends to call. He says he wants a phone for safety reasons. Which is a dumb reason, since he never does anything remotely dangerous. He'd wear a seat belt to ride his bicycle, if he ever rode a bicycle, which he doesn't because he says bikes aren't safe.

But it doesn't matter anyway because Mom's answer to both of us is the same: No cell phones.

I know Mom's not saying it to be mean. It's just paying for cell phone service each month is expensive. Ever since Dad died, we've had to be extra careful about money. Instead of our tenth birthday party being at a cool place like the nail spa or the water park, it had to be at home. And we didn't get cell phones as our birthday presents, even though we both asked for them.

I'm not saying that birthday parties and cell phones are the reason I wish Dad were still here. I wish he were still here because he was the greatest dad in the world. He snuck notes into my backpack to give me an extra boost: "Quinn, you will ROCK the track meet today!" or "Don't worry, Quinn. You'll get them next time." He made pizza from scratch. He knew how to juggle. He gave the squeeziest hugs. And when he came home from work at the end of the day, everything just felt cozier.

I'm just saying that when something as unfair as your dad dying in a car accident happens, it seems like more unfair things keep piling up on top of it. Not having a cell phone is the icing on an unfair cake. Or whatever the opposite of icing and cake are. The worms on top of a pile of mud. The cavities in a mouth of gingivitis. It's all bad, and it makes me miss my dad even more.

But back to Madeline and her cell phone. Like I said, she comes over every morning, and over cornflakes, we use her phone to FaceTime with Bella. Bella used to go to school with us. Last year her parents decided to move, and they stuck her in boarding school. That's another unfair thing. The only difference is, this one doesn't have anything to do with missing my dad.

Madeline, Bella, and I have the timing

down to a science. Madeline gets to my house at exactly 7:25. By 7:27, we're at the table with our cereal, and we have the cell phone propped up against the box so we can both see Bella. We talk for thirteen minutes. During which time my brother is usually telling us it's not safe to talk so much when we're eating, because we might start to choke. But we don't pay any attention to him. At exactly 7:40, Madeline and I say good-bye to Bella, rinse our bowls, and head out the door. As long as we run to school (another thing Zack doesn't think we should do; walking is safer), we get to our homeroom thirty seconds before the bell rings.

Today is Tuesday, and it starts like every other day. Better than any other day, because Zack happens to be over at Old Man Max's. We're supposed to call him Uncle Max, but he's not really our uncle. He's just a random old dude who Mom's family has known forever. Calling him "uncle" would be like telling a lie, and Mom

4

is pretty obsessed with honesty being the best policy. So why is "Uncle" Max the exception?

The doorbell rings at 7:25 a.m., like clockwork. I'm already in the front hall, and I swing the door open. "Hi, Madeline," Mom says as we walk into the kitchen.

"Hi, Mrs. Cooley," Madeline replies. She pulls her phone from her pocket.

"Hang on, girls," Mom says. "Isn't the big fractions test today?"

"Yes," I say.

"Unfortunately," Madeline adds.

"So maybe you should skip the call to Bella today," Mom says. "Your brother went to Uncle Max's this morning—"

"You can just call him Max," I cut in. "I know we're not actually related—thank goodness."

"Be nice, Quinn," Mom warns.

"I'm not being mean," I say. "I'm being truthful. After all, isn't honesty the best policy?"

"Uncle Max has been in our lives for a long

time," Mom says. "He feels like family."

"Feels like family is not the same as being family, and anyway, he doesn't feel like family to me. He feels like a fake."

Mom lets out a sigh. "Well, Quinn," she says. "Your utterly real and not at all fake brother went to Max's to get some extra study time in."

"There's no evidence that Zack is actually my brother, either," I say. My eyes slide to Madeline, and I give her a little smile. In a split second, Madeline glances at Mom to make sure she isn't looking at her, and then she smiles back.

"Oh, but there is evidence," Mom tells me. "Quite a bit of it. Birth certificates and hospital bracelets, not to mention the fact that there were several eyewitnesses—including me."

"Whatever," I say. "We're already late for the call."

"Why don't you put the phone away, Madeline?" Mom says. "I'll go over the fractions with you two right now."

Madeline is clutching the phone, not putting it away. She doesn't have to say a word to tell me what she's thinking: It's totally uncool for Mrs. Cooley to expect us not to talk to Bella, like we do every day.

Here's another difference between Zack and me: He has no friends, and I have lots of them. So I know it's important for people to think I'm cool. That's how you get to keep them.

Madeline's phone begins to ring in her hand, and Bella's face flashes on the screen.

"We'll talk to Bella about fractions," I tell Mom as Madeline slides her finger across the screen to answer the call. She props the phone up against the cereal box. "Hey!" I call to my best friend.

"Hi," Bella says. "I was beginning to think you guys forgot about me."

"Never," Madeline assures her.

The three of us start out talking about regular things, like whether Bella should get bangs, and what Madeline should name her new goldfish.

Right now she's calling it "Swimmy Number Three," but Bella thinks it should have its own name, and I agree; though she thinks it should be "Sushi," and I don't think that's a good name. Poor fish might be afraid it'll end up as food. Goldilocks is a good name, or Pumpkin. I'm about to suggest them, but Mom clears her throat and says, "Excuse me, girls. Isn't there something else you're supposed to be talking about?"

I look at Madeline and roll my eyes, which is code for: I'm sorry my mom is being uncool.

"We have a fractions test," I tell Bella. "My mom thinks we need to study."

"I had a fractions test last week," Bella says. "I can help."

"That's what we hoped you'd say!" Madeline tells her, and she smiles at me, which means: It's okay that your mom was uncool, because it all worked out.

Phew.

First Bella quizzes me. "What is a half times

a third?"

"Easy," I say. "A sixth."

"Correct!" Bella says. "Now, Madeline, what is a half divided by a third?"

"Um," says Madeline. "Two-thirds?"

"Errr," Bella says, making the "wrong" sound. "It's one and a half."

"That doesn't make any sense," Madeline tells her.

"Yes, it does," Bella replies. "When you divide fractions, you have to flip the divisor, so you're really multiplying one times three, over two times one."

Mom walks over from the counter. "Maybe it's easier if we write it down," she says. She has a scrap of paper, and she writes it out:

$1/2 \div 1/3$
$1/2 \times 3/1$

"I'm going to be an actress when I grow

up," Madeline says. "I don't know why I need to study math."

"Because we all had to learn to divide fractions," Mom says. "I had to learn them. Your parents needed to learn them. Even Mrs. Daniel had to learn them. And adults like to torture kids with the same things they had to do when they were young."

"That's a terrible reason," I tell her.

"You're right, it is," Mom says. "But I'm only kidding. The reason you need to learn fractions is because it's good for you girls to be well-rounded. You may change your mind about what you want to be when you grow up, and even if you don't, I'm sure actresses use math all the time."

"Like when?" Madeline asks.

"Like when they're calculating how much to tip their limo drivers," Bella says.

"Precisely," Mom says.

"Well, I wish I never had to learn any math

ever again," Madeline says.

"Ooh," I say softly, and I bend down toward my foot.

"Where'd you go, Quinn?" Bella asks.

"Sorry," I say, rising up again.

"You all right?" Mom asks me.

"Sure, fine," I say. "I just had an itch on my foot. That's all." I wiggle my toes around inside my shoe. "Everything feels fine now."

"Good," Mom says. "I think it's time for you girls to wrap this call up and get to school."

"Bye," Madeline and I tell Bella.

"Bye," she replies. "Good luck!"

2

R ELATIVITY

"Zack, are you listening to me?" my uncle Max asks.

Zack is me: Zachary Noah Cooley, kid genie.

Yes, you read that right: I'm a genie. I found out three days ago, on my birthday.

At first it seemed like my tenth birthday would be like any other old, ordinary birthday. My twin sister, Quinn, and I had a party. Which meant Quinn had a bunch of friends there, practically every girl in the fifth grade. And I had four friends. If I'm going to be honest here, I'm not sure all four counted, since I was related to three of them—my cousins Will and George, plus Uncle Max.

The only one I wasn't related to was Eli Parish.

Quinn said Eli came to the party because he's the new kid in school and he didn't know any better. I told her she was wrong, but I'm not entirely sure about that. Why would Eli want to be friends with me if no one else wants to? Not that it matters to me anymore, because now I know I'm a genie.

I'm a genie!

I'm a genie!

I'M A GENIE!!!!!!!!!!!!!

Right after the birthday party, Uncle Max came into my room with my present. It wasn't night-vision googles like I'd asked for. It wasn't even regular swimming googles. Or anything having to do with googles.

It was a bottle.

An old, scratched-up green bottle. I have to admit, at first I was pretty disappointed.

Okay, REALLY disappointed.

But then I learned it wasn't an ordinary bottle. It was a portal for genies. The word PORTAL was even written on the bottom. That means entry point, like a doorway. The genie mode of transportation.

After he gave me the bottle, Uncle Max broke the news that I'm a genie. He is, too. It's no surprise, since we're so much alike. We both wear our hair long and floppy. We both think Quinn is WAAAAAAY too obsessed with her friends from school. And we both have a birthmark on the big toe of our right foot. It's called a genie bite, and it takes a different shape depending on what age you'll be when your genie powers emerge. Uncle Max has a wavy circle, which means he was fourteen. Mine is a squiggle and a dot, which means ten. That's pretty young to have your powers emerge. I guess that means I'm a *genie-us.*

Genie-us. Noun. A genie who also happens to be a genius.

I know that word isn't actually in the regular dictionary, but it should be. One day I'm going to write a dictionary of my own.

But for now, I'm really busy with genie stuff. Uncle Max didn't get to explain much to me before my toe started to itch. Not itch a little bit like a lowly mosquito bit you. Itch like crazy, like your foot got caught in a tank of mosquitoes that hadn't eaten in a week. Or two weeks. Or ever in their lives!

I didn't know it then, but that crazy itching was a signal that I was about to be whisked off on my first genie assignment. I shrunk down to the size of an insect and got sucked into the bottle. Then I was spat out of another genie bottle in California.

California! Three thousand miles from where I live in Pinemont, Pennsylvania! I had to grant a wish for the ordinary kid who'd rubbed the genie bottle. His name was Trey, and he didn't have many friends, either. In fact I think he had fewer than I did–like ZERO. He made a wish to be someone other people liked, and I granted it.

Well, sort of. It got pretty complicated.

But there's no time to think about it now, because Uncle Max is holding my green bottle in his hands.

Not in them, exactly. His hands are cupped and it's hovering between them, like the bottle is a circle of light he's trying to contain. The letters SFG on the side of my bottle are practically glowing.

SFG stands for: School for Genies.

Uncle Max used to take me on after-school adventures every Tuesday and Thursday, but now I'll be spending those days at SFG. I'm going for the first time RIGHT NOW . . . or as soon as Uncle Max gives my bottle back.

"Zack, are you listening to me?" Uncle Max repeats.

"What?" I say. "Oh yeah. Sure."

"All right, then. What did I just say?"

"Um . . . you said . . . get ready, get set, it's time to blast off to genie school?" I guess.

"Not quite."

"You said what to do if Mom asks why I wasn't in regular school today?"

"No, I–"

"Oh, right," I say. I'd already learned this part when I was away on my first genie assignment. "When I'm traveling on genie business, the people in my real life forget about me. They forget I exist at all."

That had happened when I'd been in California, granting Trey's wish. There'd been a, uh, a *complication*, let's just say. And I'd called Mom, but when I said, "Hi, Mom, it's Zack," she didn't know who I was.

She didn't remember she had a son AT ALL.

"I don't mind missing the fractions test in school today–especially if my teacher won't even remember I exist, so I won't have to make it up," I tell my uncle. "But speaking of fractions. I just thought of a problem. You said I have SFG on Tuesdays and Thursdays. If I miss two-fifths of school every week, my grades will probably go down, and then on the days that Mom *does* know who I am, well, I don't think she'll be very happy about it."

"Zack–"

"Not that I want to miss genie school," I add quickly. "But is there some sort of special genie magic to make sure all the regular fifth-grade stuff I'm supposed to be learning gets into my brain? Like, can you snap your fingers, or tap me on the head, and get it all in there, please?"

"I don't have to," he says. "This is what I was explaining to you before. You *will* be going to your regular school every day. You won't miss a thing there."

"But then . . . how can I . . . what about SFG?"

"SFG is located in the fifth parallel," he says. "Where time hardly passes at all."

"So I'll be frozen in time when I'm there? How will I learn anything?"

"It'll feel like time is moving at its normal pace when you're there."

"That's impossible."

Uncle Max shakes his head and clicks his tongue. "How quickly you forget. Very few things are impossible, young man. Very few things indeed. Have you ever heard of relativity?"

"Sure," I say. "I know all about relatives. Unfortunately, I'm related to Quinn. But fortunately, I'm related to you."

Quinn and Mom don't even know that Uncle Max is actually related to us. The truth is, he's my grandfather seven times over. If he told everyone that, they'd be suspicious about how old he is. So he lets people believe he's just a random old guy who's been friends with our family a long time. Quinn doesn't know the truth; even Mom doesn't know the truth. Now that I do, I still call him Uncle Max. I've been doing it for so long, I'm used to thinking of him that way. Plus, we don't want anyone to see how things have changed between us, or they might get suspicious about the genie business.

"I'm talking about Einstein's theory of relativity," Uncle Max goes on. "He was a mere mortal, just like your mother and Quinn are, but he discovered that time passes slower on the moon than on the earth. If you're on the moon, you would view time there as normal, and time on Earth as passing faster. It's all relative, get it?"

"Not really," I admit.

"Rhiannon will explain it better than I did."

"Rhiannon? Is she a teacher?"

He nods. "The plan is, you'll come here on Tuesday and Thursday mornings, and then you'll head to SFG for a full day. When you come back from the fifth parallel, only a fraction of a minute will have passed, and you can be on your way to Pinemont Elementary. Okay?"

"Okay. Is it time to go now?"

"First you need your backpack."

Good thing I have my backpack ready. I

brought it with me so Mom would think I was going to regular school. I'm about to pick it up and toss it onto my shoulders when Uncle Max licks a finger and holds it in the air.

I know from experience that anything can happen when Uncle Max does that. Once he even made a dinosaur appear. Oh, and I went for a ride on that dinosaur.

But this time all that happens is a green backpack appears at my feet with a thump. The kind of thump that lets you know there are at least half a dozen textbooks inside it. I reach to unzip it.

"Wait," Uncle Max tells me. "Put your pouch on first."

"My pouch?"

He nods, and for the first time I notice something has appeared around my neck. A shiny silver rope. There's a basket hanging down at the end.

"Thanks for this," I say, wanting to be polite

about it. "But I'll just hold on to the bottle. I'm not really a necklace kind of guy."

"Is that so?"

"Yeah."

"Well, then," Uncle Max says. "You better hold it pretty tight." He unzips my new backpack for me, and I peer forward.

There aren't any books in it. There isn't anything at all. I can't even see the bottom. It looks like the sky on a night with no stars. An emptiness that seems to go on forever.

I look up and I'm about to say something to Uncle Max when I feel my floppy bangs lift from my head. I raise a hand to touch them. They're sticking straight out, toward the backpack, as if by some kind of magnetic force.

"Uh, Uncle Max," I say.

"Hold that bottle tight," my uncle says. "Use both hands."

I grip my bottle with both hands. And then–
YOW!

3

A Bird, a Plane . . . a Bumblebee Bat?

I fall into the backpack!

Actually, I am sucked into it, like someone is drinking me in through a straw. Now I'm twisting and turning and hurling superfast, like I'm moving through a maze at the speed of light. There's a rush of wind in my ears, plus my screams. I've been in genie tunnels before; but I suspect it's the kind of thing you can do a million times and still never get used to.

WHOOSH!

AHHHHH!

It seems to go on forever, and then suddenly

there's a soft thud. In the darkness, my legs are shaking, but I manage to get to my feet. The top of the backpack peels back, and I climb out. My bottle is a slippery mess in my hands. I grip it tighter and take in my surroundings.

I'm in . . . well, I'm in a room.

It's not a particularly big room, and it's not a particularly magical-looking room.

But it is a particularly GREEN room. You know how when you first wake up in the morning, you have to squint to get used to the light? This feels kind of like that, except I'm squinting to adjust to a green that's so green, it's practically glowing. The floor is covered in a lime-colored carpet. The walls are the color of an olive, or maybe closer to a pear. And to be consistent with the food theme I just made up, the drapes hanging from the window are the deep green color of a dill pickle. Even the air in the room has a greenish hue.

"Holy smokes," I mutter to myself. "This

place looks like the Wicked Witch of the West threw up all over everything."

Behind me there's a voice: "You better not let Rhiannon hear you say that. Witches need wands, and genies do not. Rhiannon would not like the observation, the connection, the comparison. Not one bit."

Rhiannon. She is the teacher Uncle Max mentioned. The last thing I want to do is upset her on my first day of genie school. I don't want to upset any of the teachers. Or any of the other kids, either. I'm determined that genie school will be different from regular school.

Of course it will be different from regular school. Regular school isn't about learning genie magic.

But there's something else I want to be different, too: I want to be popular here.

I spin around, toward the direction of the voice. But no one is there. All there is behind me is more green. Spinach green and broccoli green and avocado green. There's got to be a green door in here somewhere. Every room has a door. But I don't see one.

I'm not sure what to do. Before I get myself in any kind of trouble, I should call Uncle Max. To do that, I need to take off my right shoe and squeeze my genie-bitten toe, and a hologram of his head will appear at the top of the bottle.

I reach down for my foot. Hmm. That's weird. My shoes are different from the ones I started out in. In fact, they're not regular shoes at all. I'm wearing green slipper-shoes. Neon-green. I can't think of any food as neon as the shoes I'm wearing.

And my shoes aren't the only neon-green clothing now on my body. Gone are my jeans and gray T-shirt. In their place is a full-body suit, like a wet suit, the kind you see deep-sea divers wearing. Not that I'm about to dive into a deep sea, or a shallow sea for that matter.

At least I hope I'm not.

I'm a genie, so: I wish I'm not.

From somewhere above me, a voice calls out again. "You are Zachary Cooley, I presume?"

I look up. I look down. I look all around me. But I still don't see anyone.

"Zachary Cooley?" the voice asks, louder this time. Like whoever it is, this invisible person, is speaking into an invisible megaphone. I have a feeling that in the genie world, an invisible person speaking into an invisible megaphone is entirely possible. "Zachary Noah Cooley?"

"Yes, that's me," I call back. Not knowing what direction to face, I sort of spin around as I'm talking. My eyes dart right and left, up and down. But there's no one around. There's nothing. Well, there's green. Green, green, and more green. But nothing besides that.

Except for a tickle on my left wrist. I look down to see a little black bug–EWWW, gross! Quickly I reach over with my right index finger and flick it.

"YOWEEEEE!" the voice booms, but it seems farther away, like the roll of distant thunder. "Why'd you do that?"

The bug has buzzed back over. Though not all the way back over. It's hovering at a safe distance, so I can't reach it to flick it away again.

"Well, why?" the voice asks.

"Are you," I start, feeling a little ridiculous, because right now I'm addressing a bug. An insect. About the size of the nail on my big toe, which I suppose is big bug-wise, but as conversationalists go, it's pretty small. "Are you speaking to me?"

"Of course I'm speaking to you," the bug buzzes. "Your mouth is hanging open, you know."

I close my mouth, then open it again to speak. "I'm surprised you can speak, that's all."

"Of course I can speak. It's the only way to communicate. Rhiannon taught me the human language. Speaking to other species is her official superpower–though most other animals never learn to speak human, as I have."

"Official superpower?"

There's the sound of a deep sigh. I've exasperated the bug. "Every genie has one. An official power that no one can ever take away from you."

"What's mine?" I ask.

"Impossible to know at this point. It'll emerge on its own eventually. Although . . ."

"Although what?"

"Although I suppose there's a first time for everything–maybe you'll be the genie who doesn't have one at all!"

"No, I won't," I say defensively.

I feel all huffed up inside, and I squeeze my bottle tighter between my hands. But then I remind myself: I'm arguing with a bug.

"Time will tell," the bug says. "In the meantime, Rhiannon sent me to find you. Good thing she warned me ahead of time that you might be a handful."

"She said that about me? She doesn't even know me!"

"Still," the bug continues, paying no mind to what I've just said, "I don't think she knew you were so violent, or she would've sent me with backup."

"I'm not violent," I say, "I'm completely and utterly peaceful." If anyone is violent in my family, it's Quinn. Sometimes when I'm running down the hall to check that all the windows in our house are locked (for safety), she'll stand in her doorway and stick her foot out just to trip me. But I'd never do that. "I try to protect people from getting hurt. Truly, I do."

"Opposite of violent, huh? Tell that to my left wing."

"Sorry. I thought you were just a bug."

"Just a bug," the bug buzzes. "Humph. I am no bug, no insect, no mere mite. I'm a *bumblebee* bat. That's a mammal, you know. And another thing, I happen to have a name."

"You have a name?"

"Of course. It's Oliver-David. Not just Oliver,

and not just David. Remember that."

"Okay, Oliver-David," I say. "But . . . um . . . did you say you were a bumblebee *bat*?"

"I sure did," it says. "Why are you looking at me that way?"

"Sorry," I say, blinking away what I'm sure is a dumbfounded look. "I've never spoken to a bumblebee before, or a bat, let alone a combination of the two. I didn't even know such a thing existed."

"Clearly you were wrong."

"Clearly," I agree. "You're not at all what I would've expected."

"How's that?"

"Well, for one, you're talking. And for two, you have . . . you have *Gigantivoice*."

"I'm afraid I'm unfamiliar with that term," Oliver-David says. "Gigantivoice."

"That's because I just made it up," I say. "It's a new noun, and it means something small that has a voice that sounds much bigger than its body. I'd imagine even a regular-sized bat doesn't have a voice as strong as yours. Your voice sounds more like a lion's voice, or a bear's."

For the first time since I'd flicked it (him?) away, Oliver-David flies close enough for me to reach out and touch. Not that I would. I'm not a fan of bees, or of bats for that matter. Both are extremely dangerous.

Take bees, for starters–they can sting you, which really hurts. And if you're allergic to that sting, you can go into anaphylactic shock and die. I've never been stung by a bee before, so I don't know if I'm allergic, but it's not something I want to take a chance with.

And then there are bats, which can carry rabies. That's a very, very bad disease. If you get it, you could be a goner.

I take a step backward and almost trip over my backpack. Oliver-David flies a loop-de-loop in front of my face.

"Can I ask you something?"

"Sure you can, Zachary Cooley."

"Do you have a stinger?"

"No, I do not," he says as he flies around in a figure eight. There's a *pfft* sound, and a puff of sparkles bursts out of his butt. "Excuse me," Oliver-David says.

He farted. The bumblebee bat just *farted*; if the sparkles weren't a clue, then the smell sure is. But I've got bigger things to worry about. "Do you have rabies?"

"Of course not." *Pfft. Sparkle. Pfft.* "Now *I* have a question for *you.*"

"Okay," I say.

"Did you mean what you said?"

"What I said?" What's he talking about– all I said was do you have a stinger, and do you have rabies. I meant those questions, but now I'm wondering if he meant the answers.

"About my voice?" he prompts. "That it's really big for my size?"

"Oh. Of course I meant it," I tell him.

"Thank you. You know, I was thinking of doing some acting work, just to supplement my income."

"Your income," I repeat. "Do you need a lot of money? No offense, but back in the real world where I live, bumblebees don't actually buy things. Bats either."

"It's always good to have extra," Oliver-David says. "You never know when you're going to want something you don't have. Working for Rhiannon is a great opportunity, an honor, a privilege. I don't want to give you the impression that I'm taking anything for granted." He pauses and drops his voice an octave, like we're sharing a secret. "But I know I can do more. I worry I'm wasting my talent. And my name. It's the kind of name that should be in lights."

"Your name?" I ask. "In lights?"

"Well, of course," he says. "Oliver-David sounds like something special." He still sounds exasperated, but there's something else in his tone, too. A hint of pride. Then he adds, "I made it up myself."

"Oh, I thought it was weird that you had a name. It's less weird if you named yourself. Sort of."

"What are you talking about? My parents gave me a name when I was born, same as your parents gave to you. . . . It just didn't suit me, that's all."

"What was it?"

"That's none of your bumble-beeswax," the self-named Oliver-David tells me.

"Sorry."

"No need to be sorry, as long as you make me a promise." I nod, and he goes on. "Promise not to tell Rhiannon about my acting plans."

"Uh. Okay. I promise."

"Cross your heart, hope to die, stick bee venom in your eye?"

I thought he said he didn't have a stinger, or rabies, but just in case, I say, "Yes, I swear. I won't tell a soul. I wouldn't even have anyone to tell."

"Good, then," Oliver-David says. "Right this way."

A door opens in front of us—a door that wasn't there before. Oliver-David flies through, and I follow, turning my head to avoid his little farts. It gives me the chance to look around. We are in a corridor, a long and winding one, which is (shockingly) painted green. But not like any green I'd seen in the first room. This green is shiny, like the scales of a lizard, and light seems to dance everywhere, making it shine even more.

"You coming, Zachary Cooley?"

"Yes," I say, jogging to catch up. "Where are we going?"

"To see Rhiannon, of course."

He flies farther down the corridor, about ten yards or so away, and he turns back to shout: "You better hurry up! Rhiannon is not going to be pleased with youuuuuuu!"

I run to catch up, turning the corner after

Oliver-David. Now I'm in another big room, with shamrock-green walls that seem to stretch about a mile high. Books are stacked up against them, past what the typical eye can see. My eyes *click-click-click*, to give me the trademark genie super eyesight, and I can see the pile extends up to infinity.

"Wow," I say.

"Meow," comes a reply from below. I startle and nearly fall over a kitten weaving its body between my legs. I jump back. What if it bites? If a bite is deep enough, you could need stitches, and I have a feeling we're not near any kind of doctor's office. What if the bite gets infected? Are there any alcohol wipes in here? I don't think so. Untreated infection can lead to amputation. Better to keep my distance.

I take another step back and knock into a wall.

What?

When I turn around, the doorway that was

just there is gone. The room is sealed on all four sides, like I'm in a box. A green box. But a box nonetheless.

"At last, here you are, Zachary Noah Cooley," a voice says. "I must say, you aren't quite worth all your hype, are you?"

It's a human voice speaking, or so I think. Oliver-David has a human-sounding voice, too. Maybe it's the cat. Maybe Rhiannon is a cat. Stranger things have happened; these days they've happened to me A LOT.

I'm not sure who I'm talking to when I say, "Hype?"

"The buildup, the promotion, the antici-pation," Oliver-David says. "And I agree with Rhiannon. You're not half the man they said you'd be."

So it was Rhiannon who was speaking.

Is she the cat?

Or is she human, or something else entirely, that is invisible to my eyes? Also, I'm not half the man that *who* said I would be?

The answer comes in a flash—at least the answer to who Rhiannon is. There's a *boom* and a big spark, and quick as lightning, a desk drops right at my feet. A woman rises from behind it, holding the kitten in her arms. She's very tall, with thick hair in shades of green that are streaked with gray. It's clipped up on either side by deep-emerald-green barrettes. From the way they sparkle, I swear they're real. I feel like I'm supposed to salute, or bow, or something, so I kind of do a little of both.

The woman shakes her head to let me know I've done something wrong, and Oliver-David cackles like a witch, even though he told me Rhiannon doesn't particularly like them.

"That's enough," she says. She reaches out an arm, and I shake her hand. I feel like my body is being scanned up and down. "I'm Rhiannon. And *you're* late."

"I'm sorry," I say.

"I don't know what Max told you about SFG, but tardiness will not be tolerated."

"It won't happen again. I promise."

"Never make a promise you can't keep, young man."

"Well, I'll try my best," I say meekly.

Holy smokes, I've barely just arrived and I've already gotten myself in trouble.

"You're from the seventh parallel," she goes on, and I nod. "I know your kind, and I don't want any funny business from you."

Funny business? Does she mean like jokes? I think I'm pretty funny sometimes, but I'm not known to be a comedian or anything. There's a kid at my school, Newman, who prides himself on being a riot. I've never thought he was funny on account of him being a total *Regg*.

Regg: Noun. A kid whose parents wish they could give him back because he's such a rotten egg.

"I don't know what you're talking about," I tell Rhiannon.

"I think you do," she tells me.

"You tell him, Rhiannon!" Oliver-David cries. "He flicked my wing!"

"I didn't know who you were," I say in defense.

"Oh, so it's okay to flick a stranger, then?" Oliver-David asks. "Is that what they teach young genies in the seventh parallel?"

"No!" I say.

"That's enough," Rhiannon says. "We've spent enough time in here. Rafael, Moe, and Athena are waiting."

"Oh."

"You don't even know who they are, do you?" Oliver-David teases.

I shake my head.

"Your classmates," Rhiannon says.

"Oh, are they–" I start.

But before I finish my sentence, there's a loud *SNAP!* and we're all out of the office and in a classroom.

4

GENIE 101

The classroom is (you guessed it) green. Fluorescent green. I squint my eyes tighter and wish for sunglasses. A wish that does not come true. But my eyes adjust, and I look around.

Besides the color, it's not so different from an ordinary classroom. There's a whiteboard up front and other kids sitting behind desks. They're dressed in the same weird green wet suit that I am. But the kids themselves are different from anyone you'd find at Pinemont Elementary.

The first difference is their age. Or should I say *ages*, plural. Two of them look like they're old enough for high school, or even college. Only one of them looks like he might be ten, like me.

The second difference is that they're all looking at me.

Of course they are. I'm the new kid. When Eli Parish started at our school this year, everyone looked at him, too.

But I'm used to being *invisischool*.

Invisischool: Adjective. When everyone in school acts like you're invisible.

Invisischool is different from actually being invisible. Though I've been invisible before, too. When you're on a genie assignment, the only person who can see you is the one who rubbed the bottle.

Back at Pinemont Elementary, everyone can see me, but they don't care. They don't talk to me. They don't invite me to sit with them at lunch or pick me to be on their team in gym. Sometimes they talk about me like I'm not standing right there next to them. It's like I don't matter at all. I don't like it, but I'm used to it. That's what *invisi-school* is, and that's why it's weird now to have all eyes on me.

I look back at the kids. Then I look at the words written on the whiteboard: *Genie 101*. Then I look at the kids again.

There are only three of them, and there's no space for me. But as soon as that thought occurs to me, there's a loud snap. A desk appears. Rhiannon made it happen, no doubt. I find myself being dragged by some unseen force to sit behind it.

Meanwhile, Rhiannon takes her place at the front of the room. "We're late, so let's get to it," she says. "As you can see, you have a new classmate. This is Zack Cooley."

"Hi," I say, feeling pretty lame.

"Hey, I'm Rafael," the kid at the desk next to me says. "I'm from Brazil."

"I'm from Pennsylvania," I tell him. "That's in the United States. And I just turned ten."

"I'm eleven. It's cool to have someone close

to my age here."

"Cool."

"There's nothing wrong with us not being your age, Rafi," the girl behind him says. She brushes a fallen strand of hair from her face, and I notice her nails. They're painted the way my sister's often are. Except the paint on this girl's nails seems to shine lines of sunbeams. "I'm Athena," she says. "I'm sixteen, and I'm here from Greece."

The boy next to her introduces himself, too: "Moe, eighteen, from Myanmar."

I know most people from Brazil speak Portuguese, and in Greece they speak Greek, obviously. I don't know what language they speak in Myanmar, but I'm pretty sure it's not English.

"Did you guys learn to speak English here?" I ask. "Or is it something you learned in your countries?"

"Aren't you a self-centered one," Oliver-David says. He's been resting in Rhiannon's hair, as if he were a barrette or a bow, like the kind that Quinn sometimes wears. But now he rises and buzzes up close to me. "You think everyone should communicate in YOUR language, do you?"

"No, of course not," I say. "It's just that English is the only language *I* know."

"Look who *doesn't* know so much," he taunts.

"Some people come to us with a limited view of the world," Rhiannon tells him. She holds out a finger, and Oliver-David flies back to her and lands right on it.

"I'll say," he says.

"Does anyone want to fill your new classmate in on our method of communication?" Rhiannon asks.

"I will," Athena says. "It's Genie Auto Translate. Commonly referred to as GAT. It means when I'm speaking in Greek, you'll hear in English, and vice versa, for any human language in the world."

"Whoa," I say at the same time that

Oliver-David lets out a sigh that sounds like, "Duh."

Rafael leans toward me. "Don't worry," he says. "I didn't know about GAT on my first day, either."

Rhiannon claps her hands. "That's enough now! Zack, you're behind in much more, and you'll need to get someone's notes."

"You can share mine," Rafael says quickly, and he pushes a thin notebook toward me.

I'm glad it's small. That means there's not much to read, which means I couldn't have missed that much. "Thanks."

"And if you have any questions, just ask," he adds.

"Thanks," I say again. I glance at Athena and Moe. "Are we the only new genies in the world right now?"

"I think so. Right, Rhiannon?" Rafael asks.

"At this very moment, that is correct," Rhiannon says. "That can change at any moment, of course."

"It's weird to be in a classroom with just three other kids," I say. (And frankly, Athena and Moe don't look much like kids to me.)

"Well, what did you expect?" Rhiannon asks smugly. "Twenty new genies? Thirty? A hundred? This isn't exactly a common human condition. There are only twelve genie families in all of the world, and they don't always produce new genies at the same time."

"You mean thirteen families," I say.

"No," she says firmly. "I mean twelve. Now let's get back to work."

Rhiannon turns to the board, and Rafael leans toward me again. "I thought such a small class was weird, too, on my first day," he says.

We grin at each other, then turn our attention to Rhiannon, who has waved a finger and made words appear on the board: *The Rules of Wish Granting*.

"Who can name the big three?" she asks.

"First, contrary to popular belief, a genie assignment is only guaranteed one wish," Moe says.

"And second," Athena breaks in, "you can't change the past; you can only affect the present and the future. Third, there's no killing anyone."

"That's right," Rhiannon says. *Snap!* The words *Fame* and *Fortune* appear on the board. "Your genie assignments will wish for whatever it is they think will make them happy," she goes on. "Nine times out of ten, it'll be one of these two things. Any questions so far?"

I'm feeling totally afraid of Rhiannon, so I shakily raise my hand.

"Yes, Zack?" she asks coolly.

"Well, the thing is, when I was sucked into the bottle on my first genie assignment, the kid on the other side didn't want fame or fortune. He wanted–"

"Didn't you hear me say nine times out of ten?" Rhiannon interrupts, and I nod. Unfortunately, I can't seem to say the right thing to Rhiannon. "Did that not leave room for exceptions?" she asks.

My face flushes. "Yeah, I guess it did," I admit.

"Hold up," Rafael says. "Are you saying you already got called away on a genie assignment?"

"Uh-huh."

"No way," Athena says.

"Yes, way," I tell her.

"Before you got your genie suit?" Moe asks.

"Is that what I'm wearing? Yeah, I was in my regular clothes."

"But how'd you get in the bottle?"

"I was sucked in," I say.

The three other kids are murmuring to one another, and Rhiannon claps again. "I didn't say you *needed* the genie suit provided here in the fifth parallel. I said it's advised. It's more aerodynamic. Like swimming with all your clothes on versus swimming in a bathing suit. The water would soak into your T-shirt and pants, socks and shoes, and weigh you down. Now let's–"

"But genies don't get wet," I say. Rhiannon shoots me a look, kind of similar to one I've seen from Quinn when I'm talking safety measures. It means: *Shut up.* "Sorry," I say. "I learned that on my assignment."

I close my mouth, ready for whatever lesson Rhiannon has to teach. But Rafael leans over to me again. "Really?" he asks. "You went swimming on genie assignment?"

I glance over at Rhiannon before I answer.

"Oh, go ahead," she tells me. "I'll give you five minutes to fill them in on your first genie assignment. And if you take a second more, I will be using some magic to settle everyone down."

Everyone's eyes are on me, which is making me nervous. But I'm excited, too. This must be how Quinn feels when her friends gather around to hear what she has to say. I've never felt this way before.

I take a deep breath and start talking–quickly, so as not to go over the five minutes. "The first thing that happened was a tingling sensation shooting through my whole body, like the feeling of your foot being asleep, except this was all over. I got shrunk down as small as Oliver-David."

"Harrumph," Oliver-David says. I ignore him and keep going.

"I was sucked into the bottle, and it felt like being on a roller coaster. Not that I've ever been on one of those. If you ever read the roller coaster accident statistics, I'm sure you'll stop riding them, too. Eventually I was spit back out of a whole other bottle, and I had to figure out where I was and who my genie assignment was."

"Excuse me," Athena says, "but isn't it obvious who the genie assignment is?"

"There were three kids in the room," I told her. "Two of them were beating up the smallest one. He turned out to be my assignment. I followed them outside to a Dumpster, where they threw him. He was kind of banged up but okay. He made a wish to be someone who people liked. No one liked him. Not even his roommate. So I guess Trey's wish was about happiness, like Rhiannon said, because he must've thought he would be happier if people liked him. But it wasn't about fame, and it certainly wasn't about fortune–his family was very, very rich. He kept telling me about it. You should've seen how fancy his school was, and his father and grandfather practically paid for the whole thing to be built."

"Two and a half more minutes," Rhiannon warns.

"Right, anyway, I turned him into my twin sister, Quinn. Not on purpose. It just happened automatically. She's not a genie, but she is the most popular person I know. . . ."

"So when you got home, was your sister gone?" Athena asks. "Did your parents miss her? Oh, and–can you ever go back to visit her again?"

"I don't think Quinn would've wanted me

to go back and visit her. We aren't exactly best friends. But my wish ended up undoing itself anyway."

"Wishes undo themselves?" Moe asks.

"I don't think they're supposed to," Athena says.

"They're not," Rhiannon tells her.

"Yeah, I messed up," I admit. "I lost sight of my bottle. My bottle on the other side, I mean. You get sucked up in one and spat out another, and you're not supposed to let it out of your hands."

"Except here, right, Rhiannon?" Rafael asks. "There's a force field around SFG."

"Correct. It's one of the few places in the world."

"There wasn't one at Trey's school. There was just so much to keep track of on my first assignment, and I messed up. Then Linx from the thirteenth parallel used it as a portal and–"

"All right, Zack," Rhiannon says. "Time is up."

"He didn't even get to the part about swimming and not getting wet," Rafael protests.

"They were sprinklers," Rhiannon tells him.

"How did you know?" I ask.

"I'm the head of this school," Rhiannon says. "Do you honestly think there's anything about geniehood that I don't know?"

"I hadn't really thought about it," I admit. "But no one can know everything."

"I can," she says.

5

Fame & Fortune

Rhiannon's arm sweeps back to the words on the whiteboard. "Your genie assignment may make it easy on you and make the wish very specific. For example, a few years back I was called to grant a wish for a young miner in Sacramento. That was the beginning of what is now known as the California gold rush."

My hand shoots up, and Rhiannon reluctantly calls on me. "A few years back?! We read about the gold rush in history at Pinemont Elementary– it took place in the eighteen hundreds!"

"Time is relative," Rhiannon says.

"But that's not a matter of time moving faster or slower in different dimensions," I say. "It was . . ." I try to do math in my head. "Well, it was a really long time ago."

"For me, it feels like a blink," Rhiannon says.

"Are you the one who put the gold there?" Athena asks.

"Everything comes from somewhere," Rhiannon tells her, though I can't figure out if that means yes or no. "Tell you what, let's stay in the California region and do another example."

In a snap, the lights dim again and the whiteboard is a movie screen. An old man appears. Not Uncle Max old, but regular old. Like maybe seventy. At first he's a tiny speck, but he's walking closer and closer, getting bigger and bigger, until he's life-sized and he steps off the screen. It's like a 3-D movie, but we're not wearing special glasses. The man is so close now, I could reach out and touch him. And I do. He shakes me off. "Well, excuse you," he says.

"Sorry, I didn't think you were real," I tell him.

"Didn't think I was real?" the man repeats.

"Thomas," Rhiannon cuts in. "Please tell the class your life story in fifty words or fewer."

"Not much to say," Thomas says. "Nothing much has happened. There's only one thing I've ever wanted, and that's to be an actor–a successful actor. My wife thought I should get a real job, one that paid the bills and our kids' college tuition."

"You got married and had kids," Athena says supportively. "So things definitely happened for you."

Thomas shakes his head. "My wife got a job on the East Coast. I didn't want to leave Hollywood, so she took the kids and left me. Last I heard, she married someone else. My kids grew up and have lives of their own. Me? I'm the same. I'm still waiting for my big break."

"And your wish would be?" Rhiannon

prompts.

"I've made so many sacrifices," Thomas says. "I wish it would all be worth it."

Rhiannon snaps again, and Thomas freezes in place. "So," she says to the rest of us. "What are some ways to grant this wish?"

"Easy," Moe says. "Make him famous."

"And how might you do that?"

"Send him on an audition for an important movie role. Better yet, make it so he doesn't even have to audition. He can just be, I don't know, taking his dog for a walk or going to the supermarket for broccoli, or something. And a movie director sees him and thinks he's the absolute perfect person for the role, and he casts him on the spot."

"But then wouldn't Thomas get that role instead of someone else?" Athena asks. "What if there's another guy auditioning who really deserves it?"

"That's the point of rubbing a genie bottle,"

Moe tells her. "You get to have the good thing happen to you."

"But that means someone else is disappointed. That's not fair."

"There are probably lots of people who didn't get the part in the movie," Rafael points out. "If it was that big of a role, a lot of people must've auditioned."

"I just don't like the idea of taking the part away from someone else who deserved it," Athena says. "The person who would've gotten it if genies didn't exist at all."

"Here is something you need to remember," Rhiannon says. "When you grant someone's wish, you are not just affecting that individual life. You are affecting the world. Because that person will act differently from this point forward."

"I never thought about it that way," Moe says.

"That's why you're here," Rhiannon says, and she snaps Thomas away.

I raise my hand, and Rhiannon calls on me. "Was Thomas a real person?" I ask.

"As real as you or I."

"So when he goes home . . ."

"When he goes home, he won't remember anything that happened today," Rhiannon says. "It'll be as if he never met us at all."

"So he just goes back to his regular life of not being famous, out there in California?"

"There are a lot of unfulfilled wishes out there. People wishing for fame or fortune, like our friend Thomas here, who may never see their wishes fulfilled. And there are worse examples— people who are hungry and wish for food, or who are sick and wish for medicine. Their wishes never come true, either."

"But that's awful!" Athena cries. "What's the point of having magic if we can't fix those things?"

"We do what we can, but we can't do everything. Now, let's move on. What do you do when your genie assignment wants a new talent?"

Rhiannon snaps her fingers, and instantly there's a girl at the front of the room telling us her wish to be an Olympic athlete and win a gold medal for rhythmic gymnastics. And after her, there are a dozen more telling us their dearest wishes. Rafael had given me his notes from the days I'd missed. Now I take out a notebook that has appeared in my backpack. I take a ton of notes, more notes than I've ever taken in a class before. The pages of my notebook seem to be unending. Every time I think I'm about to flip to the last page, there are more pages. My hand doesn't grow tired, and my pen doesn't run out of ink. I think of the thin notebook I've borrowed from Rafael, and I realize the size of a notebook can be deceiving. I have a feeling that there's a lot to catch up on. But there's no time to worry about it, because I keep writing and writing and writing some more.

Finally, it's time for lunch. Instead of heading out the classroom door and down a hallway to a cafeteria, Rhiannon snaps and the front wall of the room disappears. A bunch of picnic tables are revealed. They're empty, but pretty soon dishes start popping up: rice and dumplings, a hamburger with all the fixings, fondue, a plate of sushi, lobster straight off the grill.

"Fish stew!" Rafael exclaims. "My favorite." He plops down and pats the spot on the bench next to him. "Zack, order some food already and sit with me."

"Order food?" I ask. "Like at a restaurant? I don't see any waiters."

"Just think of what you want and it'll appear," Moe tells me.

A bunch of things pop into my head at once, and pretty soon the table is piled with mac and cheese, corn on the cob, those mini hot dogs my aunt Diane had at her wedding, fudge brownies, guacamole, fajitas, three-bean salad, a ginger-bread house, and the pièce de résistance: pizza with frosting on it.

"Yum," I say at the same time that Moe says, "Disgusting."

"I guess it's a bit *yumsgusting*," I admit.

"I'm sorry, GAT doesn't seem to be working for me right now," Athena says. "I can't seem to understand that word you just said."

"*Yumsgusting*?" I ask.

"Yeah. Maybe there's no Greek word for whatever you're saying."

"I doubt it," I say. "I just made it up. *Yumsgusting*. Adjective. When something is yummy and disgusting at the same time." I pause. "But I do think I ordered a bit too much."

"Don't worry," Rafael tells me. "My first day, I ordered enough food to feed the entire country of Brazil. You'll get used to the magic."

I eat until I'm stuffed, and then I reach for more, just because it all tastes so good, but Rafael is pulling at my arm.

"Come on, guys," Moe calls. "Rafael, we need you."

Off in the distance is an old playground. "It looks so . . . so ordinary," I say. And it does: There's dirt and grass and some pretty tall slides. Too tall if you ask me. "Did you know every year at least two hundred THOUSAND kids are injured on playgrounds?" I ask Rafael. "I bet the stats are higher for slides as tall as these."

But Rafael doesn't answer. He's raced ahead, and now I can see him in the distance, pressing his hands into the dirt. I wonder why. Is it some kind of genie game? Or is this what they do where he comes from?

There's a rumble and then a *whoosh*. Rafael jumps back as the dirt turns to water. Tons and tons of water. It's spouting up from the ground like a hundred different geysers and cascading down the slides. The playground is now a water park.

"My genie superpower," Rafael says. "Water."

Moe and Athena are whooping with joy, grabbing inner tubes and boogie boards, and racing forward.

"Let's go!" Rafael says.

"Sorry," I say. "But it's too dangerous to go swimming after you eat. I think we should do something safer. Anyone have a deck of cards?"

"Nope," Moe says. He passes under an

archway of water, and his green suit transforms to swim trunks.

"Maybe Rhiannon can magically make cards appear," I say.

"I don't want to play cards," Athena says. "I want to swim."

And then she's gone, too, under the archway and into a bathing suit.

Rhiannon steps up behind me. "Is there a problem here?"

"I really stuffed myself at lunch," I tell her. "If I get a cramp, I could drown."

"Zack, you're in a water park in the fifth parallel. Mortal rules don't apply."

"Yeah, it's fine, Zack," Rafael says.

"It's just that I'm not much of a water fan."

"This is my superpower. I'll make you into a water fan!"

"No, thanks." Rafael looks toward the slides. "You go on ahead," I tell him.

I can tell he wants to, but instead he sits

down with me, back at the picnic table. They've magically been cleared, and there actually is a deck of cards there. Rafael and I play war, rummy, and snapjack. I know it sounds pretty ordinary, but there is a kind of magic going on, unlike any magic I've ever seen before. In that instant, right then, I know I've made a best friend. It's not like Eli, who was the new kid and wanted anyone to be his friend. Rafael has been here at SFG longer than I have, and even if Moe and Athena are older, he could go be with them if he wanted to. But he's not. He's choosing me instead. That's more magical than riding a dinosaur, if you ask me.

Before I know it, Rhiannon blows a whistle and announces that we are done for the day. Moe and Athena drag themselves out of a huge wave pool. "Amazing," Athena tells Rafael.

"Yeah, thanks, man," Moe says. "You two should join us next time."

Rafael glances at me. "We'll see," he says.

Athena and Moe are already dried off and

back in regular clothes. "Say your good-byes," Rhiannon says, and before the word is even out of my mouth, I feel a pull toward the backpack, and in seconds I'm back in Uncle Max's house. He's standing by the coat hooks in the front hall, exactly where I left him. It's as if I never left in the first place.

"How are you?" Max asks.

"Fine," I tell him. "Great! I made a friend. His name is Rafael. He made dirt turn into water. Plus, I talked to a bat, because Rhiannon tamed him, or something like that. I don't think she likes me, but–"

Max holds up a hand. "There's nothing I'd like more than to hear all about your first day, Zack," he says. "But you're back here in the human world, and time is moving forward. You have to get to school now and take that fractions test. Come back at three o'clock. I'll be waiting, and I want to hear everything."

6

FRACTIONS

*S*PLAT!

So this is my life. I'm a genie. I get to go to *GENIE SCHOOL*. Then I'm thrust back into mortal life, and I end up facedown in the hallway outside Mrs. Hould's classroom.

Mrs. Hould is my fifth-grade teacher at Pinemont Elementary. Fortunately, Pinemont has a rule against twins being in the same classroom, so Quinn is across the hall in Mrs. Daniel's classroom. She isn't here to see this, or I'd never hear the end of it from her.

Unfortunately, there's no such rule keeping

Reggs out of my classroom.

And the biggest Regg of all is standing over me.

"Hey, you, watch where you're going," Newman says. There's a smirk on his face, and he's trying to look all innocent, but I know he just tripped me on purpose.

My books are scattered across the floor. Eli Parish gathers them up and then extends a hand to help me stand.

"I'm fine," I tell him.

I'm better than fine. I'm a genie who just got back from genie school, for crying out loud.

None of them know the truth about me, but if they did, things sure would be different. Newman wouldn't be tripping me in the hallway. He'd be offering to carry all my books for me. But I wouldn't let him. I'd turn him into a snail. Or something worse than a snail. A slug. Something that needs mucus to survive and doesn't even have a shell to protect it. "You don't have any idea what I could do to you," I tell him.

"Oh yeah?" Newman says. "What's that?"

"I can't tell you."

"Oooooh," Newman says. "I'm so scared that I'm shaking." He looks over at Eli. "You're picking the wrong kid to be friends with. But if you come to your senses, you should come over after school. Matt and Dylan will be there, too."

More Reggs.

"Uh, well," Eli says, shifting his weight from one foot to the other. "I don't know."

"All right, boys," Mrs. Hould says, walking up between us. "Stop hovering in the hallway and come inside, please."

I take my seat in the last row. The good thing about the last row is that no one sits behind you, so I don't have to worry about Newman or any of the rest of them throwing things at the back of my neck. Genies should be able to make force fields around them, just like how there's a force field around the fifth parallel.

Maybe we can. Maybe that's something I'll

learn how to do at SFG on Thursday.

But right now it's only Tuesday morning, here in Pinemont, Pennsylvania, and Mrs. Hould passes out our fractions test. I make myself hit pause on the genie thoughts so I can focus on the task at hand.

1. A large pizza pie at Primo Pizzeria has eight slices. You have three-quarters of a pie left, and you want to divide it evenly between four people. What does everyone get?

Mrs. Hould likes us to show our work in the margin, so I draw a pizza and divide it into eight slices. Then I black out two of them, because that's the quarter of the pie already eaten. Six slices left. Six for four people. That doesn't sound fair. I should use some of my genie magic to make the two missing slices reappear! Magic! Presto! Pizza for everyone! I snap my fingers without thinking about it.

"Zack Cooley," Mrs. Hould says. "Please keep your eyes on your own page."

"My eyes were on my page," I say quickly, feeling my cheeks redden.

"Eyes on your page, and hands on your pencil," she says.

Okay, fine. I pick up my pencil and try to concentrate on the task at hand:

$6/1 \div 4/1$

When you're dividing fractions, you have to flip them:

$6/1 \times 1/4$

That's the same as six divided by four, which is one slice, with two slices left over. Each person gets one whole slice plus half of another. Next question.

2. You have twelve donuts and you want to give a third of them to your friend Betty. How many donuts does Betty get?

I start drawing fractions in the margin again, but then my mind wanders back to being a genie.

A genie and a regular kid.

Genie. Regular kid.

Half the time I'm someone magical who has the power to change lives. And the other half of the time I'm just "hey, you, watch where you're going" to a bunch of Reggs. Half and half, speaking of fractions. Or maybe not half and half. Maybe it's a third and two-thirds, or a quarter and three-quarters, or some kind of fraction that's too hard to calculate but that matters a whole lot more than the ones printed on the paper from Mrs. Hould.

After all, what good will multiplying and dividing these numbers do me when someone out there could be finding a bottle right now–RIGHT NOW! RIGHT THIS VERY NANOSECOND!– rubbing it, and then whisking me away on a genie assignment.

Maybe it would be someone like Trey, wishing to be liked.

Or maybe it would be someone like Thomas, wishing for fame and fortune.

Most likely it would be someone I've never heard of before, wishing for something I've never imagined. It would be up to me to make it happen and make sure I don't mess up anyone else's life in the process.

It's such a hard thing, being a genie. You have a lot of power, which is definitely cool. But that kind of power comes with a lot of responsibilities. I didn't appreciate that when Uncle Max first broke the news to me, but now it's the number one thought racing around my brain. If my next genie assignment happened to rub the bottle right now, would I be ready for it?

I don't know. I hope so.

One thing is for sure, though. If it happened right now, this test would never get done. And if you want to know the truth, that wouldn't bother me at all. Not one bit. I wish my life wasn't in fractions. I wish I was a genie all the time.

"All right, students," Mrs. Hould says. "Please put your pencils down now, and pass your papers to the front of the room."

I look down at my paper. I'm pretty sure I

got the first question right. But the rest of it is just scribbles of fractions that don't make sense. I flip my paper over and hand it up to Eli, directly in front of me.

"I won't go to Newman's after school if you don't want me to," he says. "In fact, maybe you could come over instead. I have a card trick to teach you."

"Sorry, I can't," I say. "I have to go to my uncle's after school."

"Maybe tomorrow, then," he says.

"Tomorrow I'll probably be busy, too," I say. "I'm sorry, Eli. It's nothing I can explain to you because you wouldn't understand anyway, but you should feel free to make other friends. I think Newman is right about my not being the right friend for you."

"I don't think he's right about that," Eli says.

"All right, Zachary Cooley and Eli Parish," Mrs. Hould says. "That's enough chatter. Take out your science textbooks, please."

7

A Phone Call

Uncle Max is in the kitchen when I slam into his house. The teakettle is on the stove. He has pulled a step stool over to the sink, and he reaches for one of the mugs hanging on a hook by the window.

"I'm here!" I say. "I have so much to tell you!"

"Patience, my boy," he tells me. "Why don't you sit down? I'll be with you in a few minutes."

I take a seat, drumming my fingers on the kitchen table as I watch Uncle Max place the mug on the counter. He steps down from the stool and opens a cabinet to get out a regular glass. He pours half seltzer, half orange juice into the glass as the teakettle begins to whistle. Uncle Max takes his time, putting the seltzer and juice containers back in the fridge. Then he turns down the flame on the stove and lifts the kettle to the mug. The steam rises in swirls. I swear the whole thing is happening in sloooooow mooooootion.

Uncle Max adds milk and sugar and brings the mug, along with the glass, over to the table. "Here you go: fizzy orange juice, just the way you like it."

"Thanks," I say.

Uncle Max sits across from me and takes a sip of his tea. "Ahh," he says. "Still a bit hot. I need to wait a minute or two."

"Why don't you cool it down with magic?" I ask. "And why did you make the tea like a regular person would in the first place, instead of snapping your fingers and making it happen? I'm sure you could if you wanted to. You'd never have to wait for the teakettle to boil again! You'd never have to use the step stool! You'd never even have to flavor anything with milk or sugar or wait for anything to cool! It'd be snapped right into perfection!"

"That's all true," Uncle Max says. He glances out the window that looks onto the backyard. There's a hummingbird at the bird feeder. I watch its wings flapping at least a dozen times a second. That feels like my heart right now, beating excitedly in my chest with thoughts of everything happening in my life right now.

"You could do things faster than that bird out there," I tell Uncle Max. "Why don't you?"

"Life is about balance," he says. "I want to make sure you don't lose sight of that as you begin your genie journey. Speaking of which, how was your fractions test?"

"Fractions, schmactions," I say. "Who cares about them?"

"I'm sure your teacher does," Uncle Max says. "And I'm sure your mother cares that you learn them, too. As do I, as a matter of fact."

"It was fine," I say. "It was a regular old fractions test. But I've been waiting all day to tell you about SFG, and there's nothing regular about that. Don't you want to hear about my first day?"

"Of course."

I have a hand on my glass, but I never lift it to my mouth. Instead, I just talk and talk until I tell Uncle Max everything–and I mean EVERYTHING–the words spilling out FASTER than a hummingbird's wings. Faster than the speed of light. Faster than the tunnels between here and the fifth parallel.

"I made a friend," I say. "And not just any friend. A best friend. I think he's a best friend, at least. He feels like one. He hung out with me instead of being with the other kids. It's not at all like Eli Parish, who's only my friend because he's a new kid and doesn't know any better."

"I'm sure that's not true, Zack," Uncle Max says.

"It is true," I admit. "Quinn was right. But it

doesn't matter, because I have Rafael. It's so cool to have a best friend."

"Yes, I know," Uncle Max says. His voice is wistful, and just like that, in the time it takes to snap your fingers, I stop feeling happy for myself and feel sad for him instead.

"You used to have a best friend, too, didn't you?"

"I did," Uncle Max says. "A long time ago."

"Is he dead now?" I ask. Uncle Max is old–really, really old. I don't know his exact age, but he's certainly older than any other person alive, unless they're genies, too. But maybe he once had a best friend in school, who grew up and lived a regular amount of time.

"No, no, he's not dead," Uncle Max says. "But things change, as you know. My brother, Linx, changed."

A chill runs up my spine at the mention of Linx's name. He's not dead. He's just banished to the thirteenth parallel. I wish he were dead. That way he wouldn't scare me so much. "I'm not talking about a sibling who was your best friend," I tell my uncle. "When Quinn and I were little, we were like best friends, too. Then we grew up a little bit. Quinn found her friends in school. It was easy for her and hard for me. I used to wonder why, but now I know: I wasn't supposed to be best friends with a regular person. I'm supposed to be best friends with a genie. With Rafael. You were right, what you said."

"I often am," Uncle Max agrees with a smile. "But what was I right about this time?"

"When you first told me I was a genie, and I said I didn't want to be. You were right about the power and the value. It's bigger than anything I'd ever dreamed of, and it–"

Uncle Max lifts a finger. "Hold that thought," he tells me. "Your mother is calling."

"No, she's not," I say. "The phone isn't even ringing."

But the instant the words are out of my

mouth, the phone does, in fact, ring. Uncle Max stands and reaches for the receiver. "Hello? Oh, hi, Dana."

"Mom, I'm going to stay here for dinner!" I shout toward the phone. I haven't actually asked Uncle Max if that's okay with him, but I know it is.

I also know, without even hearing Mom's voice, that there's a problem. I can sense it through the phone, like I'm somehow tied into the telephone wires connecting Uncle Max's house to my house right now.

"What's that about Zack's foot?" Uncle Max says into the phone. His eyes flash to mine. My foot. My toe. My genie bite.

"My foot is fine," I say.

"His foot is fine, Dana," Uncle Max says into the phone. "Why?"

I hear Mom's response through the phone: "Quinn is complaining about an itchy toe. It sounds a bit like what Zack felt on his birthday.

It's probably a bug bite or athlete's foot."

"I'm sure you're right," Uncle Max says. His voice is calm, but his face doesn't look calm at all. "Say, I've been thinking. What if we do a family dinner tonight? It's been a while since I made my famous veggie meatloaf. . . . Don't worry about the ingredients. I have them right here."

There are no ingredients right here. But it doesn't matter. As soon as he hangs up with Mom, he snaps his fingers, and our used cups fly toward the kitchen sink, landing with soft thuds. I hear the faucet turn itself on, rinsing them.

Max is already headed to the front door. "Wait," I call from behind him. "I'm sure it's nothing to worry about. Regular people get itchy feet all the time. Quinn could have a bug bite, like Mom said. Or athlete's foot, whatever that is."

"Athlete's foot is a fungus," Uncle Max tells me.

"Ha ha ha," I say. "Quinn has a fungus."

"I think you of all people should know that

it's wrong to make fun of someone for something they can't help."

I feel my cheeks redden. He's right, I should know that. Because there have been plenty of times that kids in school have made fun of me.

"But Quinn can't be a genie," I say. "Remember on Saturday when I called her to tell her I was, and it came out sounding like nonsense to her? If she really were a genie, she would've understood what I was talking about."

"We'll get to the bottom of this," Uncle Max says. "Now get your backpack–and don't forget your bottle."

The front door pops open without him touching the handle or even having to snap his fingers to make it happen. He ushers me out. "Quinn is your twin. *My* twin and I were linked by our genie bites." Uncle Max shakes his head, and his long scraggly hair flops from one side to the other. "I just don't understand. I checked you both when you were born. When I saw the genie bite on your toe, I double-checked Quinn's. In fact, I triple-checked hers."

"I've never seen any unusual marks on her foot," I add. "Unless you count the weird nail polish she and her friends sometimes use. I don't get it. We all know what your toenails look like. What's the point of painting them?"

"One of life's great mysteries," Uncle Max says.

"But she doesn't have a birthmark," I say. "I know she doesn't."

"Unless it's invisible," Uncle Max tells me.

"An invisible birthmark?" I ask. "But it's a mark. It HAS to be visible. Otherwise it's not a mark at all. That's against the rules."

"A genie bite is a magical birthmark," Max says. "And magic doesn't always follow the rules."

"Listen," I tell him. "Quinn can't be a genie. That's MY thing."

"You've only known about it for three days," Uncle Max says. "That's hardly cornering the market on geniehood. And you're not the only genie in the world, as you well know."

"Fine," I say. "It's not only my thing. It's yours, too, plus Rhiannon's, and Rafael's, and the other students'. But not Quinn's."

"Why does it bother you so much if she's a genie, too?"

"Because . . . because . . . because being a genie is my whole life, and now Quinn is just gonna swoop in and ruin it."

"It's not your whole life. And it won't be Quinn's, either. But I think it may be a *part* of her life–and there's only one way to find out."

"Ugh," I say. "I just want what's mine to be MINE. And what's Quinn's she can keep. It's not like I want to share her *slame* friends."

Slame. Adjective. Same kind of lame as Quinn.

"It doesn't work that way, Zack," Uncle Max says. "The world isn't divided into mine versus yours. And if Quinn is a genie, then it is more

89

important than ever that you get along."

"It's not my fault we don't get along," I argue.

Uncle Max holds up a hand. "This is not about fault, Zack. This is about moving forward. Now let's go to your sister."

8

Doctor Max

We haven't used any genie magic to get from Uncle Max's house to mine, but it doesn't take very long anyway, since we only live a couple of blocks away from each other. I pull out my key to open the door. I don't know what Mom is going to say about the fact that we don't have any groceries with us. Maybe Uncle Max is counting on her forgetting that part of their conversation. But just before we step inside, he gives a quick head swivel to make sure no one is looking and snaps his fingers. Bags full of meatloaf ingredients materialize in his arms. Of course. Why didn't I think of that?

Mom meets us in the foyer and takes the bags. "Umph," she says. "These are heavy. Zack, you didn't let your uncle carry all this by himself, did you?"

"Um. He didn't ask me," I tell her.

"You should *offer* to help people," Mom tells me, shaking her head. "Not wait for them to ask for it. Especially Max. He is so good to you, and you are younger and stronger than he is."

"Not to worry, Dana," Uncle Max says. "I'm stronger than I look." When Mom turns to head into the kitchen, he gives me a wink. "Now, where's the patient?"

"Quinn!" Mom calls.

Uncle Max sits at the table, while Mom and I unpack the groceries–she insisted that he sit down and relax and that I help her. Then Quinn walks into the room. "Hey, nut job," she says, whacking me on the back of the head.

"Hey!" I say.

"Quinn, lay off your brother," Mom says. "And say hello to Uncle Max."

"Hi, Max," Quinn says. I know she leaves out the "uncle" part because as far as she knows, he's just an old friend of the family, not an uncle at all. I can't argue with her on that, because of course she's right about him not being our uncle. But she has no idea what he really is to us.

But Mom gives her a Look, because she thinks Quinn needs to respect Uncle Max more. Quinn steps up to the counter and shoves a baby carrot into her mouth.

"Hi there, Quinn," Uncle Max says. "Your mom tells me you're having foot trouble. I'm sure it's nothing, but why don't you sit here and let me take a look?" .

"No, thank you," Quinn says.

"Quinn, come on. Let him take a look," Mom tells her.

"Why?" Quinn asks. "He's not a doctor."

"That's where you're wrong," Mom says.

"What?"

"Uncle Max was an army medic."

"Are you joking?" Quinn says.

"It'd be a weird thing to joke about, wouldn't it?" Mom asks.

"Well, but then how come I haven't heard about it before?"

"It was a long time ago," Uncle Max says. "Before your mom was a little girl."

"When was it again, exactly?" Mom asks.

"Oh, I don't remember specific dates," Max tells her. "When you've been around as long as I have, the details tend to blur." He pats the seat next to him. "Come on, Quinn. Let me take a look."

Quinn shoves a couple more carrots into her mouth. Then she reluctantly walks over to where Uncle Max is sitting. She kicks off a pink sequined moccasin and lifts her right foot up onto the chair. "So as you can see, *doctor*," she says, "it looks perfectly normal."

"No, it doesn't," I tell her.

"What are you talking about?" Quinn asks. She sits down and lifts her foot onto her lap, examining it herself. "There's nothing wrong with my foot," she insists.

"You're right," I say. "It's the body the foot is attached to that makes it look abnormal."

"ZACK!" Quinn says, jumping to her feet. She looks like she's ready to punch me.

"Enough, both of you," Mom says. "In all the books I read when I was pregnant, it said twins share a special bond. But these two . . ." She lets her voice trail off, shaking her head at Uncle Max. "Well, I wish it was like what the books say."

The second she says the *W*-word, I get a little tingle on my toe. It's not a bad tingle. Not at all like it was the day I found out I was a genie, when if I'd had a wish of my own, I may have wished for my whole foot to disappear. Okay, I wouldn't really ever wish that, because having two feet is a useful thing. But that's how bad that feeling used to be.

And it still is for Quinn, apparently. She thumps her bare right foot on the floor: *THUMP THUMP THUMP.*

"Quit that, Quinn," Mom says.

"I can't help it. This itch on my toe is driving me crazy."

I look at Uncle Max, and he gives me a slight nod. I know what it means: No doubt about it, Quinn is a genie.

"It's worse than ever," Quinn goes on. "I just know I caught something from Zack because he's the only person gross enough to give me a foot disease. All the kids in school know it. That's why he has no friends. I wish I weren't related to him."

"I wish I weren't related to you, either," I say.

"YOW!" she says, and she drops to the floor.

"Quinn!" Mom cries, rushing around the island in the kitchen. But before she can get to Quinn, Uncle Max snaps the fingers on his right hand. Right there and then, Mom freezes in place.

9

FAMILY BUSINESS

Mom isn't the only thing that's frozen. Everything else is, too. Everything except Uncle Max, Quinn, and me.

The water Mom was using to wash veggies in the sink has frozen midstream. The second hand on the clock above the stove has frozen midclick. Outside the window, a bird flying up from the ground with a piece of string in its beak has frozen midflight, its wings bent like the letter *M*.

"Oh no!" Quinn cries. "Mom!" She runs toward her and tugs on her arm, but Mom doesn't budge. She's like a mannequin in a store.

Or a statue. "Mom! Mom! This isn't funny! Come on!"

"She's going to be okay, right?" I ask Uncle Max.

"I don't know if you're talking about your mother or your sister," he says. "But they're both going to be fine."

"Phew."

"Mom!" Quinn calls. "What's happened to you? Please, Mom. *Please* wake up. I need you!"

Uncle Max puts a hand on Quinn's shoulder, but she swats him away. "Don't touch me!" she snaps.

"Quinn, listen to me," Uncle Max says. "You don't need to worry. I promise."

"Trust him," I tell my sister.

Quinn spins away to grab the telephone on the counter. She presses the button to turn it on. She presses it again and again and again before banging it on the counter. "I can't get a dial tone! What is happening?"

"Let me explain it to you, Quinn," Uncle Max says. "Your brother and I are genies. Do you understand the words I just said?"

"Now is not the time to tell me some fairy tale!" Quinn screams.

I looked over at Uncle Max. "She understood your words," I told him.

"Yes," Uncle Max said.

"But the genie bite," I say. "She doesn't have one. Doesn't that mean it's impossible for her to be a genie?"

"You know what I think about that word," Uncle Max says.

"Very few things are impossible," I recite.

He nods. "Very few things indeed."

If I'd learned anything these last few days, it was that he was right. But when you've spent ten years thinking certain things to be true, like dinosaurs no longer exist and that genies have never existed, it's very hard to wrap your brain around the endless possibilities of it all.

"Of course I understood his words," Quinn yells at me. "Now tell me what's going on! Tell me the TRUTH!"

"He IS telling you the truth," I say. "We ARE genies. That's why my foot itched so badly at our birthday party. It wasn't an invisible bug bite, like I thought. It was because Madeline–"

"Don't drag Madeline into this!"

"I'm not dragging anyone," I say.

I turn to Uncle Max and give him a look like *Do you see what I mean about her?*

"I've got to get out of here!" Quinn cries. "I've got to get help for Mom! Maybe you don't care, but I do!"

"Of course I care. She doesn't need any help."

But Quinn ignores me and runs to the door. I run after her. "Quinn! Stop! Wait up!"

But she yanks the front door open and runs off, almost falling over our neighbor, Mrs. Landman, who apparently was out walking her pet poodle, Ernie. Both Mrs. Landman and Ernie are frozen. Poor Ernie was caught midpoo. It's stuck in the air, halfway between Ernie's butt and the ground, and it's a pretty gross sight to see. Even Quinn stops short to do a double-take, then looks away in disgust.

Uncle Max comes up behind me. "Quinn," he calls. "It's okay if you want to run off for a while. I understand. I'm sure your brother does, too."

"I do, Quinn. I really do," I say.

"But I've frozen time," Uncle Max continues, "and the sooner you listen, the sooner everyone can go about their business."

"And Ernie can *finish* doing his business," I add.

I don't know if Quinn got the joke. But she reluctantly shuffles back into the house, being careful not to step too close to Uncle Max or me. We follow her toward the kitchen. She looks at Mom, and I can see the way Quinn is looking at her that she's about to start crying.

"He's going to snap her back to normal," I

say. "You just have to listen to him first."

Quinn gives Mom a last look, then she turns to Uncle Max. "You have three minutes to explain yourself," she tells him. I don't know what she plans to do once the three minutes are up. And I don't know how she intends to keep track of time, either, since none of the clocks in the house are working.

Holy smokes! I bet none of the clocks in the entire world are working!

"All right," Uncle Max says. "You know how I have known your family a long time—"

"Yeah, yeah," Quinn says. "We're not really related at all. But what's that got to do with anything?"

"Ah, Quinn," Uncle Max says. "But we *are* related. I'm your great-grandfather seven times over."

"But that would make you . . . I don't know exactly, but it would make you too old to be alive, so that's impossible."

"My dear Quinn, as I just told your brother—very few things are impossible. Very few things indeed. It was my genie powers that allowed me to freeze time so I could tell you about this." He slips off his right shoe to show Quinn his genie bite. "This isn't an ordinary birthmark," he tells her, wiggling the toe with the wavy circle on it. "It's a genie bite. Zack has one on his toe as well, albeit a slightly different shape. I checked you both when you were born, and you didn't have one. So I thought the genie powers had skipped you. But it seems you are one, too."

Quinn shakes her head. "This is crazy," she says softly.

Her eyes slide toward Mom. I can almost see the thoughts churning in her brain: *It can't be true, but if it isn't true, how is Mom standing like a statue?*

She goes from shaking her head to pinching herself up and down her arm. "I feel it, I feel it, I feel it," she mutters.

"You're not dreaming," I tell her as she reaches out and pinches my arm–hard! "OW! What'd you do that for?"

"I needed to make sure," she says. "Plus, I needed to punish you for knowing this since our birthday and not telling me."

"I couldn't tell you!" I say. "It's Genie Board Decision . . . number . . . number . . ."

"Two hundred and fifty-eight," Uncle Max supplies.

"Right," I say. "The fact that you can understand what we're saying proves that you're a genie. Or else it proves that you're my genie assignment. That happened on our birthday. You see, this kid named Trey rubbed the bottle and he made a wish to be someone that other people liked. And you popped into my head because you have a lot of friends. Then Trey went to the bathroom, and when he came out–"

"You know what, Zack?" Uncle Max says. "I think this is a lot more information than Quinn needs right now. Remember how overwhelmed you were when you first found out?"

"Yeah," I say. "And then I was thrown into the deep end on my first day, and I had to know everything."

"Be that as it may, I haven't even given your sister her bottle yet."

Snap! Suddenly he's holding a scratched-up bottle in his hands. Like my own bottle, it has the letters SFG engraved on the side, along with the number seven and the word PORTAL on the bottom. But this one is for my sister.

"Here," he says to Quinn, handing it forward. "It's a genie portal, a kind of doorway. When your genie assignment rubs his or her bottle on the other side, this is how you'll reach them."

"It's like traveling through someone's lower intestines," I break in. "At warp speed."

"I got this, Zack," Uncle Max says. He looks back at Quinn. "You following so far?"

"This is totally bonkers."

"It only seems that way," he says. "But when the time comes, you will shrink down to fit in this entry point. And until then, you need to hang on to this. There are genies out there who'd like to get their hands on it, and that would be bad."

"Very bad," I say.

"Very bad indeed," Uncle Max agrees. "I wish I could protect you from the evil forces in the world, but I can't. You have to protect yourself."

The way Quinn is holding the bottle in her hands, it looks like she doesn't even know what it is. Like it's something that just landed in her hands from outer space. Which, I guess, in a way it did.

"I don't understand any of this," Quinn says.

"That's normal," Uncle Max says. "Perfectly normal. It takes time for it to sink in. You can put the bottle in your room now, but don't leave the house without it. And don't let it out of your sight when you're out of the house."

"I'm supposed to carry a bottle around for

the rest of my life."

"On Thursday, you'll join Zack at SFG, and I think that will help."

"School for Genies," I tell her. "Isn't that cool? I have a best friend there. His name is Rafael."

"Do you have any questions, Quinn?" Uncle Max says.

"Mom?" Quinn says, her eyes sliding toward our mother, still frozen in the middle of the kitchen.

"I'll snap time back," Uncle Max says. "Remember, your mother can't know anything about this conversation. Even if you want her to, she can't know."

"Okay. Just make her come back."
SNAP!

10

BACK TO SCHOOL

I gotta be honest. I am NOT thrilled to have my sister join me at SFG. Of course I don't have a choice. I'm a genie–that's the good news. But my sister is a genie, too–and that's the bad news.

She agrees that it's bad news, and here's some more honesty for you: It makes me a little bit happy that she's unhappy. If she was all *Woo-hoo, I'm a genie! Watch me now!* that would make it even worse. It still feels a little bit like just my thing, because she doesn't want it to be her thing.

But it IS her thing.

And on Thursday morning, we're on our way to Uncle Max's together. The first stop on the way to SFG. Quinn is, predictably, moaning and groaning about it.

"Madeline always comes over for breakfast with me. She doesn't even have the cereal she likes at her house."

"Boo-hoo for Madeline," I say.

"You just don't care about her because you don't have any friends."

"I do so," I tell her.

"You care about Madeline?"

"What? No. I don't want anything bad to happen to her, but I'm not worried about her breakfast situation. But I mean, I have friends."

"Just Eli," Quinn says. "And you know he doesn't really count."

"I'm not even talking about Eli," I say.

Quinn holds up her hands and makes a *W* with the thumbs and pointer fingers. "Whatever," she says.

Uncle Max told Mom he needed our help moving some boxes, and Mom believed him. She has no idea there are no boxes, and even if there were, Uncle Max could move them with the power of his genie mind. She thinks poor Max is too old to do things on his own, and she was more than happy to lend him Quinn and me. "Don't let Uncle Max lift anything himself," she said as Quinn and I headed out. "He's much frailer than you both. But you should also be careful. If a box seems too heavy, take some books out, or carry it together."

Uncle Max's house is in sight now. "And don't expect me to move any boxes," Quinn goes on. "I don't care how old Max is. As far as I'm concerned, it's his fault I have to deal with this stupid genie thing–and there shouldn't be free hard labor on top of it!"

"Relax," I tell her. "There aren't going to be any boxes."

"There aren't?" she says. "Then why did he

tell Mom there were? And if he lied about the boxes, then I bet he lied about this genie thing, too. I knew it was bonkers. Didn't I tell you it was bonkers?"

"Yeah, yeah," I say. "But you're wrong. He just made up the boxes thing so it'd make sense to Mom that we were going over there this morning. But then . . ." I let my voice trail off. "I guess I shouldn't tell you."

"But then what, nut job?"

"But then, he wasn't really lying. It's all part of genie initiation. You're going to be lifting boxes full of boulders by yourself ALL DAY!"

"ZACK!" she screeches, and she lunges for me, but I'm too fast. There are no more streets to cross, so it's safe to run the rest of the way to Uncle Max's. I'm not even panting when I get to the front door. Must be my *glungs*.

Glungs. Noun. Amazing genie lungs.

But Quinn trudges the rest of the way, as if moving in slooooow moooootion. Uncle

Max waits for her in the doorway, and when she finally climbs the porch steps, he is all smiles. "Welcome, Quinn," he says. "I'm so glad you're here. The first day at SFG is an exciting day for every sparkie."

"Sparkie? What the heck is that? You're calling me names now? Just so you know, in the human world that's not considered a very nice thing."

"No, it's not," I say. "So why do you call me nut job all the time?"

"Because you are one," Quinn says.

If Mom were here, she'd tell Quinn to knock it off. But she's not, so I look to Uncle Max, knowing that surely he'll tell Quinn that kind of thing isn't allowed. Not when you're a plain, ordinary human, and not when you're a genie, either.

But he says nothing of the sort. Instead, he explains what a "sparkie" is, and how it's not really a bad name at all: "A sparkie is a genie, like you, who has just learned about her powers. I know it's still new enough to be a shock. I've been a genie for more years than I've bothered to count, and it's still a shock sometimes. But it's also a privilege. Maybe you don't see it now, but you will. I think you're going to have a wonderful day."

"I know *I'll* have a wonderful day," I interject. "Because I get to see Rafael again. He's my new best friend."

"Well, how nice for you," Quinn says. "You have a best friend for the first time in your whole miserable life. I have about half a dozen best friends, and I didn't need to be a genie to meet any of them."

"Quinn," Uncle Max says, and for a split second I hold out hope that he's really going to let her have it now. But nope. Instead he goes on, "I'm sure you're going to make some wonderful friends, too."

Another thing I gotta be honest about:

Uncle Max is being awfully nice to Quinn, when she really doesn't deserve it. I know the genie thing is tough to swallow at first. I wasn't too crazy to find out about it myself. But she's never been nice to him, and he's acting like she's his very best friend. Or at least his favorite between the two of us.

Not cool, Uncle Max. Not cool at all.

"Let's just get this over with," Quinn says.

"Very well," says Uncle Max. He opens the door wider for Quinn to step inside. Once the door shuts behind her, two backpacks land with a thump at our feet. *Thump*, a backpack in front of me. *Thump*, a backpack in front of Quinn.

"I'm not carrying that," Quinn says.

"You don't have to," Uncle Max says. He's holding a silver rope in his hands, which he slips over Quinn's head. At the bottom is a pouch.

"And what the heck is this?"

"It's for your genie bottle," I tell her. "Duh."

"Zack," Uncle Max says, "I don't know if the

'duh' was necessary. On your first day, you didn't know what it was for, either."

Now it's my turn to say "Whatever."

My own pouch is snapped into place, bottle inside it. I hear Uncle Max starting to instruct Quinn on what to do–"Step inside, and hang on, because–" But I don't hear the rest, because I've unzipped my own backpack and stepped inside. Just like that, I'm gone.

WHOOSH!

ZOOM!

EEEEEEEEEEEEEEEEEEEEEE!

The twisting and turning goes on forever, and then suddenly I land with a gentle thud, back at SFG. I step out of the backpack into the World's Greenest Room.

"Zachary Cooley, you have returned, I see," a voice buzzes around me.

"Of course I'm back, Oliver-David," I say. "It's Thursday, and there's nowhere else I'd rather be. But you don't need to bring me to class. I know the way."

Thud.

A cucumber-colored bag lands next to me, and Rafael pops out. "And even if you didn't know the way, I'd take you," he says.

"Hey, thanks," I say.

"No prob," he says, giving me a fist bump. It's a Newman thing to do. I've seen him fist-bumping the Reggs before–usually after they've done something to humiliate me. But I don't mind that Rafael is making the same gesture now, because he's making it to *me*. I've never had someone to fist-bump before.

"That's all very well," Oliver-David says. "That's fine. That's dandy. But it is another Cooley I am here to meet."

"Another Cooley?" Rafael asks.

"C'mon," I say, taking off down the green hall. "I'll race you to class. Last one there is a rotten sparkie."

Rafael and I get to class at the exact same

time, and I take my seat right next to him. Within seconds, Moe is back in his seat, and Athena is in hers. Rhiannon is at the front of the room.

And before long, Quinn is there, too. Oliver-David buzzes over and rests on Rhiannon's shoulder. Quinn stands at the front of the room, looking every bit as confused as I felt two days ago, on my first day at SFG. And there's something else in her expression—anger.

But no one else seems to notice.

"Whoa, another new kid!" Moe says. "Two in one week. That's got to be some kind of genie record."

"Welcome," Athena adds.

"Class, this is Quinn Cooley," Rhiannon says.

"Quinn Cooley," Rafael repeats. "Another Cooley." He turns to me. "You mean, this is your sister—Quinn?"

"Yeah," I admit.

"I thought you said your sister wasn't a genie."

"She wasn't," I say. "And now she is."

"And she needs a seat," Rhiannon says. "So we can all get started."

"She can sit next to me," everyone seems to say at the same time. Everyone but me, that is. And it's not that I don't want Quinn to sit next to me. Okay, fine. I don't. But more than that, I know Quinn doesn't want to sit next to me, either.

"Let's see, where shall we put you?" Rhiannon says.

I'm making a wish of my own: *I wish Rhiannon puts Quinn anywhere but next to me.*

"I helped Zack on his first day," Rafael says. "So I have experience helping new kids."

"Very well," Rhiannon says.

And anywhere but next to Rafael, I add.

But my wish doesn't work. I shouldn't be surprised. Genies don't make wishes. They grant them. With a snap of Rhiannon's fingers, I feel my chair slide across the floor, away from Rafael. Then *poof!* A new desk pops up right between us.

"There you go," Rhiannon tells Quinn.

NOOOOOOOOOOOOOOOOOOO! I cry. But it's a cry in my head, not out loud.

"You can borrow my notes if you need them," Rafael tells my sister.

"Thanks," she says.

Rafael smiles at her, and Quinn gives him a little smile back. So this is how it's going to be. First Uncle Max is being all nice to Quinn without her even deserving it, and now she's taking Rafael from me, too.

"All right, let's get to the first lesson of the day," Rhiannon says.

But I've already learned my first lesson of the day: When it comes to best friends, it's easy come, easy go.

Leave it to Quinn to ruin everything.

11

It's Me, Quinn. I'm Back Again.

"My, Quinn, you have grown up since I last saw you," Dr. Grantham says. "Why don't you sit down and catch me up on your life."

She says the word *why*, which is a word you use if something is a question and the other person has a choice.

But it's not a question, and I don't have a choice.

Mom made me come here. She left work early to pick me up from school and drive me over, even though I told her she didn't have to. I told her talking to Dr. Grantham wouldn't help at all. But Mom picked me up and drove me over anyway, and now she's sitting in the waiting room outside Dr. Grantham's door.

Dr. Grantham is the psychiatrist Mom sent Zack and me to right after Dad died. Mom thought talking to someone outside the family would make us feel better. I know I said wanting cell phones was the one and only thing my brother and I ever agreed on. But actually there's a second thing: No amount of talking to a stranger about Dad will make us feel better about him being gone.

Anyway, here I am now, back in Dr. Grantham's office, for reasons that have nothing to do with my father.

"Your mom tells me you've been talking in a secret language," Dr. Grantham says.

"It's not a secret language," I tell her. "It's just words she can't understand."

"Is it something you learned in school?"

"No," I tell her.

"Do your friends know it?" she asks.

I feel heat start to rise to my cheeks at the mention of my friends. When I tried to explain to them what was going on, it came out as nonsense, just like Old Man Max and Zack told me it would. I shouldn't have said anything to them in the first place, but it's really hard to believe that the words you're saying don't sound like real words as they leave your mouth. Madeline and Annie looked at me like I was insane.

And that's a big problem for me, since you can't be insane and popular at the same time. It's just not possible.

Very few things are impossible, Max said.

Well, I bet he wasn't popular when he was in school, but he's wrong about this one.

"No, my friends don't know it," I tell Dr. Grantham.

"It's not something you're studying in school?"

"We don't start Spanish till sixth grade, and

123

that's not a secret language. Millions of people around the world speak it."

"I see," she says, and she makes a couple of notes on the pad of paper in her lap. "Did your dad speak any foreign languages?"

"My dad?" I ask. "What's he got to do with anything?"

"Sometimes when we lose someone who we love, we try to do things to connect with them. When I was your age, I had a pet dog that died. His name was Bucky and I loved him very much. We studied the constellations in school, and I found out there was a star called the Dog Star. Every night I'd look out my window and think of Bucky. I'd say good night to him before I went to sleep."

"That's nice," I say. I'm trying to be polite, even though losing a dog is very different from losing a parent. Everyone knows pets don't live forever.

Parents don't, either, but they're supposed

to live a lot longer.

"Maybe you're trying to find a way to speak to your dad," she prompts. "A language no one but the two of you can comprehend."

"No, that's not it," I say.

"So tell me what it is."

"I can't."

"Sure, you can."

"No, I can't," I say, "but it's okay."

"Of course it's okay," she says. "You're more than okay. You're doing very well under the circumstances."

"You know the circumstances?" I ask.

"Your dad's death," she says. "Your mom having to work longer hours. It's a lot to adjust to."

"Oh yeah, that," I say. "I'm adjusting just fine. In fact, I think I'm cured."

"You weren't sick to begin with," Dr. Grantham says.

"Right," I agree. "Everything is perfectly normal."

I won't talk nonsense anymore, because I won't talk about being a genie anymore. I will just be a regular kid like I've always been. Better than regular: popular.

Popular kids aren't different, which means they aren't genies. Which means I'll just ignore it and pretend it didn't happen. Maybe I made the whole thing up, anyway. It's totally, completely, utterly bonkers.

"Can I go now?" I ask Dr. Grantham.

"I won't make you stay," she says. "But we have the whole hour."

"It's fine," I say, standing and moving toward the door. "Maybe you can even give my mom her money back. I don't need any help anymore."

12

QUINN'S SECOND DAY

The next Tuesday is Quinn's second day of genie school, my third. This time Max told Mom he bought a dog, and he needed us to walk it a couple of mornings a week–Tuesday and Thursday mornings.

"I bet he doesn't even have a new dog," Quinn grumbles.

"Of course he doesn't," I tell her. "But that's all right. We don't have time to walk a dog. We have to get to SFG!"

"The fact that you think this is all so great just proves that you're a nut job."

"The fact that you don't proves that YOU are."

It's not my best retort. Still, I know it's true.

"I don't understand it," I go on. "If anyone should feel bad about going today, it's me. My first day was great, but then you showed up and you were everyone's favorite. Rafael wanted to sit next to you, and Athena magicked your nails so they looked like hers."

Quinn lifts up a hand to examine it. The polish shines like sunbeams.

"Even Moe liked you. Everyone liked you. You weren't being all that nice, and they still did. I don't understand it."

I'll never understand popularity. Kids who aren't nice sometimes get it, like the Reggs and Quinn. And kids like me who never did anything mean to anyone, well . . .

"I'm missing Madeline again right now," Quinn grumbles. "She went to Annie's for breakfast. She did it on Thursday, too. What if she starts liking it better there and has breakfast with Annie EVERY day?"

"Then you'll just see them both at school. It's no big thing."

"You wanna know why you don't have friends, Zack? It's because of this."

"Because Madeline likes having breakfast with Annie?"

"Because you don't realize how important it is to be there for your friends. You have to be the kind of person who shows up and who's in the right place at the right time."

"But how do you know the right place?"

Quinn shrugs. "I just do. And I know that the right place for me to be right now is with Madeline, and since I'm here with you instead, I'm missing out."

And with that, we've reached Uncle Max's door. Unlike last time, he's not standing out front, waiting for us. I ring the bell. No answer, so I put my hand on the doorknob. It's locked, but the instant my hand touches it, I feel the lock slide. "Whoa, amazing," I say, pushing open the door.

"Not so amazing," Quinn says. "Plenty of people leave their doors unlocked. They don't think everyone in the neighborhood is out to rob them."

"Uncle Max," I call into the house, ignoring Quinn. "Uncle Max?" Through the front hall, into the den. No Max. The kitchen, the living room. Nope. I race up the stairs, but he's not in his room. The bathroom door is wide open, and there's no Max.

Now my heart rate is picking up speed. Where could Uncle Max be? Outside? Why isn't he answering? Is he hurt? I know he's a genie, but I can't stop being scared.

"Zack!" Quinn calls.

"I can't find Uncle Max!" I call back. "Not that you care."

She comes toward me, waving a piece of

paper in my face. I take it from her, and read Uncle Max's curly script:

Dear Zack & Quinn,

I was called away on genie business, but you two know what to do. Your backpacks are in the mudroom. Have a great day at SFG. I'll see you upon your return.

Love,
Max

"He's not even here!" Quinn exclaims.

"When you get called up for genie business, everything happens very fast," I say. "I'm surprised he had time to leave a note." I pause, thinking. "It must've happened right before we got here, otherwise Mom wouldn't have remembered he existed. Mortal humans, like Mom, forget us genies exist when we're off on genie business."

"Well, I don't think I should have to go to

genie school if Max isn't even here to make me. Madeline and Annie are probably on the phone with Bella. If I go to Annie's right now, I can FaceTime, too."

"You're really afraid to miss talking to her ONE TIME?"

"Two times," Quinn says. "This is the second time. Thursday will be third, and next week it'll be fourth and fifth. It all adds up. Right now they can be deciding what our colors of the season will be, and I won't get to vote. Or maybe they'll plan a party and forget to invite me."

"You have FOMO," I tell her.

"This stupid genie stuff has interfered with my life enough."

"The genie stuff is not stupid," I say. "It is real life. It's the other stuff that doesn't count."

"The other stuff is my whole life," she says.

"Fine," I tell her. "Don't come to SFG. Just leave."

"Oh yeah," she says. "Like you'd really let

me leave. If I tried to do that, you'd freeze me the way Max froze Mom."

"I won't," I say. "I don't want you to come, anyway. It's better for me when you're not there." While talking, I've walked into the mudroom to get my backpack, because no matter what Quinn thinks, I certainly don't want to be late to SFG. I see our two backpacks on the hooks. Twin backpacks for twin genies. I reach for mine and unzip it.

"Well," I say, "are you coming or going?"

"If I have a choice, I'm definitely not going with you."

"Okay, see you later," I tell my sister. I now know better than to lean into the backpack. This time, I open it up as wide as I can, jump up, and–

WHOOSH!

Seconds later I land on my feet in the hallway of School for Genies. I flip my hair off my face and straighten my shirt. "Hey, Zack!" I hear someone call behind me.

"Rafi! Hi!" I say.

"Where's your sister?"

"She's not coming today."

"She's not? Is that allowed?"

I shrug. "Whether it is or it isn't, she didn't care. She stayed home. She doesn't want to be a genie."

"We don't have a choice."

"I know. She's still a genie. She'll just be a really bad one."

"Huh. I thought she liked it here."

"Come on," I tell Rafael. "You still have me. And we don't want to be late for class."

13

THE BEGINNING OF EVERYTHING

Class begins without my sister. I know she's supposed to be here, but frankly, her absence is putting me in a better mood. Rhiannon asks after her, and I shrug just the same as I did to Rafael. "She doesn't want to be here," I say.

"That won't do," she says, and she snaps. I'm afraid that means she's just summoned Quinn, but instead words pop up in the air: THE HISTORY OF GENIES. "Let's get started. It is time to discuss how genies came to be. The beginning of everything. Turn around."

We turn as she snaps a second time. The

back wall of the classroom disappears, and there is the planet Earth spinning before our eyes. Spinning *backward*.

"Years ago–nay, *eons* ago," Rhiannon tells us, "on the first day of the first month of the first year in history, the first genie was born."

The planet comes to a halt, and Rhiannon points to a place in the center of it. We zoom in closer, to a field of grass and a little baby lying in the center, laughing. He is lifting a toe to his mouth–a toe with a red genie-bite birthmark.

"And at that very moment," Rhiannon goes on, "there were eleven others born around the globe. Twelve genie originals, scattered across the planet Earth. They looked like the other humans, spoke like them, lived among them. But as you know, they had a few special things that set them apart. As each of the originals came of age, those special powers became known."

Moe raised his hand. "How did they become known?" he asks.

"Much the same way that anything is discovered," Rhiannon says. "Trial and error. Long ago, there was someone who was the first person to rub two sticks together and figure out that made a fire. Someone else was the first person to realize you could put wheels on something and push it along. And there was a first genie to be summoned into a bottle to grant a wish."

"Where did the bottles come from?" Athena asks.

"The original bottles washed up on the shore," Rhiannon says. "No one knows how or why. It's the mystery of why any of us are here. As new genies are born, new bottles are discovered, and they make their way here. We mark them."

"SFG," I say, rubbing the letters on my own bottle.

"Yes, and when a genie comes of age, he or she is given a bottle, their portal, to grant wishes."

"Are any of the original twelve genies still

alive?" Athena asks, which is something I've been wondering about, too. Uncle Max is old. Really, REALLY old. When I first found out I was a genie, I was afraid that meant he was about to die and I was supposed to take over. He said it didn't work that way. So then I'd asked if genies lived forever, which almost seemed worse. I didn't want to watch everyone else I knew and loved die before me, but he said it didn't work that way, either. Then I was sucked up into the bottle on my first genie assignment, and he never did get around to telling me what way it actually *did* work.

Rafael raises his hand. "My great-great-great-great-aunt told me there are some originals left," he says once Rhiannon has called on him.

"Yes," Rhiannon says. "I've heard that, too. Though none of us really know who the originals are. What we do know is this: Genies age slower than regular humans. It's a little bit like when we look through the window at the earthly world, and things appear to be frozen. They're not really frozen. They're just moving a lot more slowly. That's how a genie ages. It happens. It's just happening more slowly."

"But isn't that the opposite?" Athena asks. "Shouldn't we be aging faster if time goes by quicker up here?"

"Everything has its own clock," Rhiannon says. "Now let's move on and talk numbers."

There's a snap at the front of the room, and we all turn back to a whiteboard that has just appeared. The numbers appear on their own: *12.*

"Mortals think the number twelve is significant for many reasons," Rhiannon says. "The twelve months of the year, the twelve cycles of the moon. Anything else significant about the number twelve?"

"Twelve genie families!" Rafael calls out.

"Yes."

"I have a question," I say. "I know you said there were twelve originals. But there's really thirteen. So when did that happen?"

"It didn't," Rhiannon tells me. "You are mistaken."

"No, I'm not," I insist. "This is what I started to tell you on my first day. My genie assignment was going just fine, and then–"

"I thought you said you accidentally turned your genie assignment into Quinn," Moe breaks in. "That doesn't sound just fine to me."

"Okay, so it wasn't," I admit. "But the real disaster was when Linx showed up."

"The guy from the thirteenth parallel?" Rafael remembers.

"Yes, the thirteenth family in the thirteenth parallel."

"Nonsense," Rhiannon says. "There are twelve families and there always have been."

"But Linx broke off into a thirteenth family," I say. "I think he used to be in the seventh family. I'm not sure. But he must've been, because he's my uncle's twin brother."

"Speaking of twins," Rhiannon says, "you didn't do a good job of keeping track of yours."

"Quinn wouldn't listen to me even if I wanted her here," I say.

"She's a flake, a flit, a truant," Oliver-David adds.

"I like her," Rafael says.

"Yeah, well, she only likes her other friends," I say. "She wanted to hang out with her friend Madeline instead, so I left her at my uncle Max's house. I'm sure she's still frozen there. I mean, not frozen exactly. But you know, moving very slowly, since time is relative."

"Is that so?" Rhiannon asks. Before I can reply, she's snapped a window into place in the front of the room. The shade is already up, and we can see directly into Uncle Max's mudroom. Quinn's backpack is still hanging on a peg. Quinn herself is turned away from it, facing the door.

"She looks just like you," Athena says. "I noticed that the other day."

"She does not," I say.

"They're twins," Moe says. "What'd you expect?"

"We're not identical," I say. "For one thing, I'm a boy and she's a girl. And for another, we have completely different personalities."

I don't even want to look at Quinn anymore, and I'm turning away from the window when something catches my eye. Her bottle, which is on the bench under her backpack, is starting to glow. Faintly at first, but then brighter and brighter.

"Do you see that?" Athena asks.

"How can things be changing if they're basically frozen still?" Moe asks.

As soon as he says that, it disappears. *Poof!* Gone!

Oliver-David begins to shout. "Rhiannon! Did you catch that? Did you witness? Did you see?"

Something is happening to Quinn. She's changing, too. Her body is sparkling. No, not sparkling. It's disappearing. First her feet, then her legs, her body, her head. Faster than I can say Quinn Frances Cooley, she's gone completely. Some speckles, like glitter, in the shape of the outline of her body are the only evidence that she was ever there in the first place.

I can feel my heart pounding in my chest, seventy times a second, twelve hundred times a minute, fast as the beat of a hummingbird's wings. Maybe even faster.

Hummingbeats. Noun. Your heart beating as fast as a hummingbird's wings.

I take a deep breath.

"Maybe it was through the bottle," I say, trying to calm myself down. "Maybe she's on her way here right now."

"No, I don't think so," Rhiannon says. "I've never seen a bottle disappear like that before. Besides, her backpack is still in the room."

It's hanging on the peg, right where Uncle Max left it.

"Maybe she was called away on a genie assignment," Rafael says.

"She would've gone into the bottle," I say. "It wouldn't have disappeared first."

"That's right," Rhiannon says. "And remember, time on Earth is moving slower than we are, so it wouldn't have happened that quickly."

We're all staring at the space where Quinn used to be, and something else is buzzing through the air.

"Is that . . . ," Oliver-David starts. "No, it can't be. I thought I was one of a kind."

"I'm afraid not, O-D," Rhiannon says.

"It's another bumblebee bat!" Athena exclaims.

"I think he's writing a message," Rafael says.

We watch the bumblebee bat's sparkle-farts curling through the air. I gasp when he's done: 13.

"Thirteen," I say. "Linx is from the thirteenth parallel. Could it be him? Or a bug working for him?"

"Bumblebee bats are mammals," Oliver-David says.

"Whatever. Did Linx take her?"

"Signs point to yes," Rhiannon says.

"But he's awful!" I say. "I mean he's truly terrible. He's going to hurt her–I know he is! She may not realize it at first. At first he makes it seem like all your dreams will come true. He takes your dearest dreams and turns them into nightmares. Like, one time, a woman wished to be beautiful and he turned her into a flower! She wasn't even human anymore!"

"No!" Athena says.

"Yes!" I cry. "He told me so himself. He was even proud of it. We need to get there before he does something like that to Quinn–or something even worse!"

"Children," Rhiannon says gravely, "I think it's time for a field trip to the thirteenth parallel."

"But I thought you said there was no such thing," Athena says.

"And even if there is, it doesn't sound like a place we should go," Moe adds.

"Genie Board Decision eighteen-oh-six," Rhiannon says. "We leave no man behind."

In an instant, there's a bottle in Rhiannon's hands, and *SNAP!* the shrinking tingles travel through me from head to toe.

"My body!" Athena screams.

"What's happening?" I hear Rafael cry.

But I don't hear Rhiannon's reply because my ears are suddenly too small to work anymore. I'm smaller than Oliver-David, and I'm buzzing, buzzing, buzzing toward the open bottle top. Rhiannon, Rafael, Athena, and Moe are right behind me. We're spinning and spinning through the room, and suddenly everything is black, and we're gone.

14

HISTORY LESSON

We're twisting and turning and hurling superfast. The other genies and I are bumping into one another like we're a pile of laundry in the dryer. When you're traveling through a wormhole at the speed of light, bumping into other people hurts A LOT.

WHOOSH!

AHHHHH!

OWWWWWWWWWW!

It seems to go on forever, but finally I feel myself start to slow down. Soon all five of us are stuck at the top of Rhiannon's bottle, competing to get out. (Six of us, if you count the mini bumblebee bat.) I'm being squeezed so tight, I swear my internal organs are getting smushed together. My lungs have been shoved into one. My stomach feels like it's being squeezed up through my mouth. I suck in my breath and try to make myself even smaller. Squeeze squeeze *squeeeeeeeeeeeeeze*. And I'm out. Phew. I'm panting, trying to catch my breath, as I float down toward . . . well, I don't know what I'm floating toward, because it's pitch-black. I can't even tell if my eyes are open.

And I'm not floating, either. I'm in free fall. Zooming faster and faster through the nothingness, until I land with a *thud*.

Ouch. That hurt. Next time I go through a genie bottle, I will wear a helmet and elbow and knee pads. But for now, I need to find my friends.

"Hello?" I call.

My mouth is too small; my voice is too faint. No one answers me.

This is the blackest darkness I've ever seen in my life. I can't make out the shapes of the other genies, or even myself. I hold my hand in front of my face. Nope, can't see it.

My body is tingling again, and then the popping starts. Even if I can't see it, I can feel it. My hands, my feet, my arms, my legs, my torso are all popping back to the regular size. There go my eyeballs, one right after the other, and my ears. My mouth is still itty-bitty, but Rhiannon must have hers back to the regular size, because she shouts out: "Is everyone okay? Oliver-David?"

"I am here," comes the shaky reply of the bumblebee bat. "But I do not feel fine at all."

"You're the only one who can see in here," Rhiannon tells him. "I need you to check on everyone else."

"I'm too scared to open my eyes."

"Do it!"

"Okay . . . yes, I see Moe. I see Athena. I see Rafael. And I see Zack."

"All right, good," Rhiannon says. "The gang is all here."

"Where are we?" Moe asks as my own mouth goes pop. Finally.

I don't need Rhiannon to answer that. "This is the thirteenth parallel, isn't it?" I say.

"Yes."

"And the gang is NOT all here yet." I raise my voice to as loud as it will go and shout: "QUINN! WHERE ARE YOU?"

"Ow, that was right in my ear," Athena says.

"Sorry, I didn't see you." I turn my head and shout again, though this time I'm not quite so loud: "Quinn!"

There's no answer.

"Quinn!" I try again. "Say something! Say anything!"

I strain my genie ears, but there's nothing.

"Zack," Rhiannon says, "I don't think she's in range right now."

"What does that mean?" I ask.

"The thirteenth parallel is larger than all the galaxies in the universe," Rhiannon says.

"Have you ever been here before?" Rafael asks.

"No, but I have heard," Rhiannon says. "We may have quite a journey ahead of us."

"How can we go anywhere if we can't see anything?" Moe asks.

"Just wait till I get a hand back," Rhiannon says.

"Oh no! What happened to your hands?" Athena asks.

"Nothing, it's just they're still small," Rhiannon says.

"Oh. Okay."

"Has any genie ever *not* gotten all their body parts back to regular sizes?" Rafael asks.

"Oh my goodness! I don't have my legs back yet!" Moe says.

"I don't have my nose! What if I never smell anything again?!" Athena says.

"Relax, sparkies," Rhiannon says. "In the history of geniehood, everyone has gotten their body parts back to regular size."

"And what about my sister?" I ask. "In the history of geniehood, have people always found their family members who went missing in the thirteenth parallel?"

"I can't say that's ever happened before," Rhiannon says. "But your family has a special connection here."

"Do you think the chances are good that we'll find her?"

"I thought you didn't even like your sister," Moe says.

"Oh, good," Rhiannon breaks in.

"What?" I ask. "Is it Quinn?"

"No, one of my hands is now back," she says. She gives a loud snap. Usually when Rhiannon snaps, things happen. Something appears. But I can't see anything, so I don't know what she's conjuring.

Snap. Snap. Snap.

"Well, that's funny," Rhiannon says.

"What?" I ask.

"My hand. I'm trying to snap up some light, but I can't."

"Maybe it isn't quite big enough yet," Athena suggests.

"No, I'm sure it is. I'm afraid it's Linx."

"Linx?!" Oliver-David cries. "He's HERE?!"

"He's somewhere," Rhiannon says. "But wherever he is, he's blocked our magic in the thirteenth parallel."

"Then how can we understand each other?" Rafael asks. "Isn't Genie Auto Translate a genie power?"

"No, GAT is not a power," Rhiannon says. "It's an involuntary function, like your heart beating, or your lungs breathing. Now, Zack, I need you to close your eyes. Tell me which way you feel your sister."

I close my eyes, even though it's so

pitch-dark, it's not like having them open was making any kind of difference. "Feel my sister?" I repeat.

"Yes, sometimes siblings have a bond that defies blocked magic."

"But Quinn and I don't have a bond," I say, my eyes popping open again.

"Then why are we here?" Moe asks.

I don't know how to answer that question, but luckily I don't have to. Rhiannon turns to Oliver-David. At least she would've turned to him if she could see, probably. Instead, she just speaks into the void, hoping he is right there listening. "O-D, you're going to have to be our eyes for a while. Tell me, what do you see?"

"I see a path," he says. "That way."

"Which way?" I ask. "We can't see anything, remember?"

"Just a ways away, a few steps."

"Everyone hold hands," Rhiannon says. "Oliver-David, lead us forward."

I grip hands with Rafael. We're moving slowly, following the bumblebee bat's voice. Have you ever gone to the bathroom in the middle of the night, and after you turn off the light to head back to your room, it's even darker than it was before? That's what this is like, except a million times darker and a million times more dangerous.

"This is kind of cool," Rafael says.

Oops. Must not be his hand I'm holding. His voice is too far away to be next to me.

"Cool?" Moe repeats. Oh, there's the voice next to me. "Nothing about this is cool. We're moving through a vast darkness."

I have to agree with him. "It's dangerous. We don't know where we're stepping. If we hit something sharp, we could need stitches, and I don't see any doctors around."

"I don't see anything at all," Moe says.

"Or we could step off a cliff," I say.

"Oliver-David won't let that happen," Rhiannon says.

"Oh, great," Moe says. "Our fate rests in the hands of the world's smallest bat. That doesn't sound risky at all."

"Hey," Oliver-David pipes up. "I'm hurt. I'm insulted. I'm offended."

"And Rhiannon didn't want to admit this place even existed," Moe goes on. "Which isn't inspiring any feelings of comfort or safety right about now."

"With Zack and his sister in our class, I probably should've put this place on the lesson plan," Rhiannon says. "I hoped Linx wouldn't be a problem. He hasn't been for a long time. But it seems the scabs of old wounds have been scratched off, and now here we are, so I'll give you a crash course. Rumor is that Zack and Quinn's great-grandfather seven times over is one of the originals."

"But that's impossible," Athena says. "A great-great-great-great-great-great-great-grand-father is certainly old, but not old enough to have been around at the beginning of time."

I agree with her about that, and some old feelings of anger start to boil up. I'd been so mad when Uncle Max told me about the genie stuff; mad because he'd kept it a secret for so long, and that's like lying. Of course it wasn't really his fault, but now I feel like I've been lied to all over again.

"It sounds improbable, but nothing is impossible," Rhiannon tells Athena, which is just the kind of thing Uncle Max would say. And just like that, the anger goes away completely. Even if he did lie, I really wish he were here right now. "When the first twelve genies were born, one of those genies was actually two," Rhiannon continues.

"You mean Uncle Max and Linx, don't you?" I ask.

"Indeed. As they grew, Max developed tremendous genie powers. Linx, however, did not."

"Linx told me that he was the most powerful

genie in the world," I say.

"Oh, he is," Rhiannon says. "Linx knows how to harness the power of others. When he and Max were sparkies themselves, Max did some things that hurt his brother and–"

"Uncle Max would never do anything to hurt anyone!" I say defensively.

"That's the Max *you* know," Rhiannon tells me. "But genies change, just as people do. Long ago, there was a great rivalry between Max and Linx, and it began because Max used his superior power against his brother. He made him feel bad for being the less powerful genie. Linx was determined to do whatever he could to show his brother that he was just as good–even better. He began to harness the power of other genies, until Max cast him out of the seventh parallel. Thus, the thirteenth family was created."

"But if he was cast out, how did he get the power he has now?"

"Anger is a powerful emotion. Once Linx

was cast out, he channeled all the anger he had for his brother, and he grew stronger. Even though he was here, biding his time, sometimes when the wind blows, you can feel him."

"He's in the air?" Rafael asks incredulously.

"But this doesn't make any sense," I say. "Uncle Max wouldn't cast out his own brother. I don't believe it!"

But there's a part of me that *can* believe it. Because there's a part of me that would like to cast Quinn out of things sometimes.

Maybe I get that from Uncle Max's side of the family.

Except right now I don't feel that way. I'm going to do everything I can to save my sister.

"Rumor has it that it took Max a long time to start a family," Rhiannon says. "A very long time."

"Oh, so that's how he can be only your seventh-great-grandfather," Athena says. "I get it now."

I do, too. But it doesn't matter. We're wasting time. We have to get Quinn. That's what I say out loud: "We're wasting time. We have to get Quinn."

"Yes," Rhiannon agrees.

"How do we even know where to go?" Moe asks.

"I'm setting a compass by the light of the invisible stars."

"Invisible stars don't have any light," Athena says.

Rhiannon starts to say something in response, but then she stops herself. "Hang on," she says. "I hear something."

15

BREATH IN MY EAR

"What is it?" Moe asks, sounding alarmed.

"Quinn?" I call out. "Is that you?"

Once again, no one answers. I didn't really expect her to. I was just hoping. Wishing, really. Genies don't get to grant their own wishes, which just goes to show you how unfair the system is. But the world is full of unfair things. And most of them I can't do anything about.

"I don't hear anything," Rafael whispers to me.

I shake my head. I don't, either, even though I'm straining my genie ears. And then, in the distance, there's a faint light.

"Look at that!" Athena cries. "Someone turned on a light!"

"Hush," Rhiannon says sharply. We're all quiet, listening to the silence again. Until it's not silent, just mostly silent, with a hint of someone– or something–whispering in the distance. No, it's not anyone whispering. Maybe it's a broom whisking across a floor.

Nope, that's wrong, too. I think it's footsteps. So faint, maybe the person is tiptoeing.

I know I don't get a wish, so I'll just beg instead: *Please, pretty please, with a cherry and every other thing in the world on top–let it be Quinn and not Linx. Let it be Quinn and not Linx.*

If Quinn walked up to us right now, we could go straight home in Rhiannon's bottle. Or not straight home. We'd probably have to stop at SFG in the fifth parallel first. But that's fine. As long as Quinn is safe. I'll be nice to her, the way Uncle Max asked me to be. I'll be even nicer than he asked. I'll be the nicest sibling there ever was. I'll sit next to her in Rhiannon's class, and I'll share my notes with her. I'll share Rafael and all the others with her.

But Quinn doesn't walk up to us.

"Oliver-David, I have a favor to ask you," Rhiannon says.

"Anything for you, my queen."

"Go check out what's there at that light."

"Anything for you—but that!" Oliver-David clarifies.

"What's the problem, Oliver-David? You've been leading us the way the whole time."

"But you were right next to me!"

"Go on, now. I don't want to ask you a third time."

"But . . . but . . . ," Oliver-David sputters. "Can't you come with me? Please, Your Greatness, Your Highness, Your Goddessness. With your genie speed, you could certainly get there faster than I can. You are the fastest, quickest, swiftest genie in all the land."

"My genie speed is useless here," Rhiannon says. "And we are wasting time." In the faint light, I watch her lift a finger. She may be out of snapping power, but she is able to flick Oliver-David away.

"Rhi-aaaaaa-nonnnnn!" he calls as he somersaults through the air.

"Report back pronto!" she calls behind him.

For a few seconds, he's gone from sight, and there's nothing, just the almost darkness. Then a speck of Oliver-David appears in the distance.

"Mayday! Mayday! Mayday!" he's screaming. "Turn back! Abort mission! Go home!"

My fellow genie classmates are clamoring for Rhiannon's bottle, even though we're all too big to fit in it now. "We can't leave," I tell them. "Not without Quinn."

"Oliver-David, please," Rhiannon says. "Tell us what you saw."

The bat is panting now, struggling to get

the words out. "A charge, a smash, a crash. A STAMPEDE!"

I think he's exaggerating. At least I hope he is. From what I know of Oliver-David, it wouldn't be out of character for him to say something was worse than it really was. But as I'm wishing it, a rush of animals comes charging at us. A bear that has two heads. A lion the size of a small house. And a tiger: "Oh no, it's the saber-toothed kind!" Moe cries.

"They're extinct," Athena tells him.

"I don't think he knows that," Rafael says.

The growls and roars are so loud, the earth shakes. No, not the earth; this place, this parallel, the thirteenth parallel. My brain wants me to run away as fast as I can. But I can't lift my legs or swing my arms to propel myself forward. The light is growing brighter, so I can see more animals coming toward us—a rhino with tusks as long as its body, a pair of hippos with teeth buzzing like chain saws, human-sized scorpions, and dinosaur-sized crocodiles. All getting closer and closer.

Rafael grabs my arm. "Zack, come on!"

I am running, but I don't know where I'm running to. Closer to Quinn? Farther from Quinn? I don't know what to do. None of us do.

"Rhiannon!" Moe is screaming. "Get us out of here!"

But Rhiannon doesn't respond to him. She is standing as still as a statue, facing the stampede, and she's humming. No, not humming. She's singing. But the words she's singing don't make any sense. GAT must've stopped working after all.

Now how will we talk to each other?

Not that I should worry about that. Talking to my fellow genies doesn't matter anymore. What matters is I'm about to be someone's dinner! Rafael, Athena, and I are running and running. Moe is ahead of us. Everyone is screaming, and screams are like a universal language. I don't need GAT to know they're scared out of their minds,

too. We are all moving as fast as we humanly can. But it's no use. I can feel one of the animals behind me–its breath is hot on my neck. I turn around, just for an instant. There's a two-headed grizzly bear right behind me. So close that if I reached a hand back, I could touch it. I face forward again, willing my body to move faster, faster.

Please. Please. Please.

But I'm no match for the bear. It jumps on me with the bounce of an over-caffeinated kangaroo. I'd take one of those right now. It'd probably bruise me up pretty good, but I don't think it'd eat me.

This bear, on the other hand–it's taller than Linx, which is very, VERY tall, taller than any human I've ever seen. There's no scale anywhere, but my best guess is this monster is at least a thousand pounds. The *hummingbeats* are back in my chest, pounding like a thousand hummingbirds–with hammers strapped to their wings. I'm turning my head this way and that, trying to avoid both of the bear's mouths. When I turn to the left, I can see Rafael stretched out inside a hippo's jaw.

MY BEST FRIEND IS STRETCHED OUT INSIDE A HIPPO'S JAW! The second that hippo decides to snap its mouth shut, poor Rafi is a goner. But I can't even deal with that right now, because there's a grizzly head panting in my ear. I turn my head to the right in time to see three cougars tackle Moe.

"GRRRRRRRRRRRRRRRRRR," the bear growls in my ear. Its breath is hot. It's going to bite my head off, I just know it. And there's nowhere to look, so I squeeze my eyes shut. I hold my breath, and I wait for the end that I know is coming at any second.

Any second now.

Any second.

16

ANY SECOND

I'm still trapped, and now I'm going to suffocate from holding my breath for so long. I exhale and shakily inhale.

EW. This bear stinks like nothing I've ever smelled before. One head smells like it has eaten nothing but rotten fish for its entire life. When I try to turn away, there's the other head, smelling like a nuclear waste garbage dump. I think I might puke–from the stench and from fear. But that's certainly not my biggest problem. No, my biggest problem is still its spiky teeth, glistening with saliva. I can hear its stomach growling. It's going to chomp me up into bear food any second.

What's taking it so long? I don't want to die, but knowing I'm about to, and having to wait for it, is the worst part.

"Please," I say out loud to the bear that's about to eat me–after all, if you can talk to a bat with a brain the size of a speck, certainly you should be able to talk to a bear with two heads and four ears. "Please, I'm only here right now to save my sister. And if you eat me, she won't have a chance."

The bear growls a deep, sinister growl.

I feel my throat getting thick with tears. "Do you understand what I'm saying?" I ask. "If you kill me, you may as well kill my sister, too."

Either the bear doesn't understand, or–more likely–it just doesn't care, because now both its mouths are opening wider, drooling in antici- pation. A large splash of saliva lands squarely on my nose. I'm too terrified to be grossed out, and I squeeze my eyes shut tight again. I know this is going to hurt. The question is, how bad and for long? I hope it's fast. I hope it bites me in the exact right place to knock me out so I don't actually have to find out what it feels like to be chewed up and swallowed.

I can feel hot tears squeezing out through my closed eyelids, cascading down my cheeks. Poor Quinn. Now she'll never be rescued. And poor Mom. She already has to live without her husband; now she'll be without her children, too.

I'm crying and crying, and it just keeps going. Maybe the bear likes to torture its victims before he (she?) eats them. Or maybe it already swallowed me up, and I'm dead. No one knows what happens after you die, so maybe this is what happens: You don't even know you're dead, and you're stuck feeling scared for the rest of your life.

Err . . . I mean the rest of your death.

Maybe that's what happens. Or maybe, just maybe, the bear feels some sympathy for me, and that's making it not want to eat me so much anymore. I like eating drumsticks and steak, but I probably wouldn't if I saw the chickens and cows sobbing beforehand.

I open my eyes the slightest of slits. The bear isn't even looking at me anymore. Both mouths are closed, and it's looking off in the distance with all four eyes . . . at Rhiannon. Around me I can see Moe in the grips of the cougars. Athena is pinned down by a lion, and Rafael is still in the hippopotamus's mouth, stretched out the length of the hippo's jawline. The hippo itself is mesmerized by our teacher, jabbering away in a language I've never heard. All the animals are.

"Alu bak manif tooooor," Rhiannon says. The words don't make any sense. I feel so hot inside the grip of the grizzly bear, and Rhiannon keeps saying her nonsense words: "Uvu hear batik shurrr cazo down."

Wait a second, two of those words weren't nonsense. I understood them.

"Setpa sep hear wuuuu down now."

Now there were three.

As she goes on, I hear more and more English words, until they're all I hear: "Hear my voice, hear my words. These are my students. Don't hurt them, please. You all have brothers and sisters. They are on a mission to save one of their sisters. Don't hurt them, please. Let them continue. Put them down. Let them go."

She pauses, and it's like the whole world pauses. My breath is caught in my throat, and my heart is still in my chest. Even the bear seems frozen for a few seconds.

And then it releases me from its grip. I land on my butt with a thud. That's gonna leave a mark . . . though I suppose it's not anything to complain about, given the mark that its ginormous teeth almost just made.

The bear has an arm extended, like it wants to help me stand up. But I'm afraid to take it. Just seconds ago, it was ready to eat me, and that doesn't exactly build trust. Besides, it's got sharp claws coming out between the digits on its paw. I shake my head. "No, thanks, I've got it," I say, on the off chance that the bear will understand me.

It growls, but it doesn't sound like a real growl. It sounds like words. It sounds like it just said: "I'm sorry. I hope your sister is okay."

It gives me a sheepish wave and begins to walk away. The lion does the same, and so do the cougars and the hippopotamus. They slink off, looking kind of embarrassed. I watch as they get farther and farther away, until they disappear completely into the darkness of the thirteenth parallel. Then I turn to Rhiannon. "How did you do that?"

"We each have a superpower that won't disappear, no matter how magic is blocked," she says.

"Like water is mine?" Rafael asks.

Rhiannon nods. "Eventually the rest of you will learn what yours are. Communication is mine."

I nod, and I mean to say something back to her like "thank you." But when I open my mouth again, instead of words, the only thing that comes out of my mouth is laughter. I don't know why, but everything is striking me as hysterical, and I can't stop.

I guess it's true what they say about laughter being contagious, because pretty soon Rafael, Moe, and Athena are laughing, too. Rhiannon is laughing so hard, she's doubled over. It goes on for a long time. It all seems so funny, how crazy this genie life is. A week ago I was an ordinary kid, in an ordinary house, with an ordinary life. Now look at me: I'm a genie, and I've just talked to a bear, who apologized for nearly eating me. Plus, my sister is a genie, too!

My sister.

Quinn.

Nothing seems worth laughing about anymore. I take a deep breath.

Then another.

And then another.

I'm feeling serious, and I guess that feeling is just as contagious as laughing is, because pretty soon everyone has quieted down. No one is even smiling anymore.

"Rhiannon," I say. "Thanks for saving us. But we still need to find Quinn."

"You're right," she says. "And in order to do that, Zack, I need you to try concentrating again. Close your eyes."

"Is this about the bond between siblings again?" I ask. "I'm sure other siblings are bonded–"

"Especially twins," Rhiannon says.

"We're not identical, though," I say. "Which makes us just the same as regular old siblings. Even not as close as that, because she doesn't like me very much."

"I still need you to do this for me. Close your eyes. Tell me what you feel."

I still don't know how I'm supposed to feel Quinn just by closing my eyes. But I close them anyway. I don't see anything besides the insides of my eyelids, which are kind of a swirly orangey-red. I don't feel anything, either, except an ache in my heart like I'm missing something really important. I'm missing my sister. It's not a feeling I know well.

Oh, sure, I've missed people before. I miss my dad every single moment of every single day. But I've never missed *Quinn*. Now I do. That doesn't mean I know where to find her.

I hear Athena gasp. Rhiannon shushes her and tells me to keep feeling. So I do, even though to be honest, the only things I'm feeling are guilt and sadness for not knowing how to find Quinn when it really matters.

A few seconds later, Rhiannon speaks again. "You can open your eyes now," she tells me.

"Sorry," I say. "I didn't feel anything. Isn't there some kind of genie magic you can do to figure out where Linx is holding Quinn?"

But Athena is grinning. "You leaned to the

left," she says excitedly. "I didn't know you could feel a person, either, but you did, Zack. YOU DID!"

"I did?"

"The Leaning Tower of Zachary Cooley," Rafael says proudly.

"Holy smokes!" I say. "Come on, then. Let's go left. There's no time to waste. QUINN, WE'RE COMING FOR YOU!"

I turn left, and I'm about to break into a run, when I pause and look back at the others. "But what if I'm wrong?" I say.

"I understand your fear," Rhiannon says. "Sometimes it's hard to trust our instincts, because there are a lot of competing voices in our head. Voices that tell us what to be excited about or what to be afraid of."

"I have a lot of voices telling me what to be afraid of," I admit.

Rhiannon nods, and in her nod I can sense understanding. "But if you can tune those voices out, and you follow what your instincts tell you," she says gravely, "then you'll rarely be led astray. Come, sparkies, let's go."

I lift my left foot, ready to move forward. But Moe clears his throat. "Excuse me," he says. "I'm sorry, but I don't even know Zack's sister. My instincts aren't telling me to walk left at all."

"Not walk," I say. "Run."

"Walk, skip, hop, let's go," Oliver-David says.

But Moe stays put. "My instincts are telling me to get back to the fifth parallel and continue on home," he says.

"That's fear, like Rhiannon said," I tell him.

"No, it's instinct," he says. "Lifesaving instinct. I'm sorry, I'm sure your sister is worth saving. But I was just nearly eaten by three cougars, and my instincts are telling me to cut my losses and return home."

"If that's your instinct, we will respect that," Rhiannon says.

Moe is avoiding my gaze. "That's my instinct," he says.

Rhiannon turns to Athena and Rafael. "And you two?" she asks. "Are you willing to keep going?"

"Oh yeah," Rafael says. "I've got your back, Zack."

"Thank you," I say.

"Athena?"

"Yeah," she says. "I have a sister at home, too. If something happened to her, well . . ." Her voice trails off, and we all look at Moe.

"Sorry," he says sheepishly. "I'm an only child. If something happened to me, how would you explain that to my mom?"

"Or to my mom?" Oliver-David asks.

"You don't have a mother," Rhiannon reminds him. "At least not one that has laid eyes on you since you were born."

"I do have instincts, though," Oliver-David says.

"And I hope those instincts are telling you that *you* go where *I* go."

"Excuse me," I say. "But my instincts are telling me whoever is coming with me to find Quinn better come soon. Time is wasting."

"Right you are," Rhiannon says. "Moe, step closer."

She holds out the bottle, and he steps closer. "It's important that you follow your instincts," she says, and in an instant, he is gone. "Zack, lead the way."

"To the left?"

"To the left."

I take a step, and then another, and then another. Rhiannon, Athena, and Rafael follow behind me. Something is shining in the mist. A sign atop a building, blinking in neon yellow and green: LINX LAND.

"As if there were any doubt," Rhiannon mutters.

We've entered into some kind of city, with buildings stretching up for miles, each one emblazoned with Linx's name. Everything is clean and brand-new looking, and there aren't any other people around.

"Where is everyone?" Athena asks.

"Maybe no one actually works here," Rafael says. "Who in his right mind would go to work in Linx Land, anyway?"

"But then why have the buildings?" Athena asks.

"His name is in lights," Oliver-David says. "Who wouldn't want that?"

"If no one is there to see your name in lights, then I don't think it really matters," I tell him.

Oliver-David lets out a fart that sparkles puke-colored green and sounds like *harrumph*.

"We're here now, aren't we?" Rhiannon says. "Let's keep moving."

We wind our way through the city streets and onto country roads, where there are no more buildings to display Linx's name. But there's another sign staked into the ground: DEAD END.

I turn to Rhiannon. "Does that mean . . . ?"

I start.

"Keep going," she tells me.

The farther we go, the more signs we see: WRONG WAY, TURN BACK, NO WAY OUT.

"I think your instincts are wrong," Oliver-David says to Rhiannon as he loops around. "We should turn right."

"Nonsense," Rhiannon says.

"But the signs–" Rafael starts.

"The signs are a sign that we're headed in the right direction," Rhiannon says. "This is the thirteenth parallel. You can't expect things to say what they mean."

Oliver-David is buzzing above us, looping in corkscrews.

"You all right up there, O-D?" Rhiannon asks him, but Oliver-David doesn't answer. "Oliver-David, don't give us the silent treatment. Are you all right?"

"What?" Oliver-David asks. "Yeah. I'm fine. Why?"

"Your flying pattern," Rhiannon says. "It's a little . . . off."

"I've never flown in the thirteenth parallel before," Oliver-David says.

"Fair point."

"If we're going in the right direction, can we go faster?" I ask.

"Yes," Rhiannon says. The four of us break into a run, with Oliver-David buzzing above us. The path has changed from a country dirt road to the mossy ground of a forest. But I'm going fast–as fast as my mortal powers will take me. This isn't genie running, but still, I feel like I'm flying. Faster, I push myself. Faster. Until I touch down at the wrong place, the root of a tree, and trip and fall. I scramble to stand back up and start running again, but that's when a branch from the tree reaches down and grabs me.

17

It's a Twig, It's a Branch, It's an ARM

Yup, that's right: A tree branch just grabbed me.

That's not an expression. That's not my mistaking someone's arm for a tree branch.

It's an actual tree branch. A splintery, knobby wooden branch as long as a king cobra snake and at least as thick. It reached down, thin little twigs at the end like fingers, and curled around me, scratching up my arms in the process. "Hold on!" I shout after the other genies, plus Oliver-David. "I'm stuck! Come back!"

By the time they circle back to me, there are three more branches—a total of four coiled around my body. I twist and wiggle, but I can't get loose. In fact, the branches are squeezing tighter, like they're the fingers of a fist. I can feel leaves on the top of my head. The tree is bending forward, closing in on me.

"Let me go!" I shout at it. "You guys, *help*!"

"Oh my goodness, Zack," Rafael says, reaching his hands toward me and yanking me by the shoulders. "You are really, seriously stuck. Someone give me a saw."

"Oh, right," Athena says, coming up beside him. "Let me just get the saw I have out of my back pocket." She pretends to reach back. "Oops, I must've forgotten it at home, along with my retractable ladder and garden hose."

"Don't joke at a time like this," Rafi says.

"Sorry, Zack," Athena says.

"Help me yank him out," Rafael tells her. "Rhiannon, we could use your muscle, too."

"The trees in this forest are stronger than titanium," Rhiannon says, stepping up beside him.

"Even if my genie powers were working and I could produce a chain saw right now, it wouldn't make a scratch."

"We had a lesson on metals in school," Athena says. "In my real school, I mean. Not genie school. Anyway, titanium is the strongest metal on earth."

"But it's nothing compared to *barkanium*," Rhiannon says. "Which is what these trees are made of." Tentatively she rests a hand on the trunk and rubs gently up and down, as if she thinks it's a nice tree to pet, not a tree that's holding one of her students hostage. Then she looks over at me. "Yes, I'm sure it's barkanium. I'm sorry, Zack."

"You're sorry?" I ask. "That's it?"

Rhiannon nods. "I'm afraid so. Unless the tree decides to let you go out of the kindness of its heart"—she gives the tree another little pet, but I feel its branches shudder around me at her touch—"there's nothing I can do."

I didn't know trees even had hearts.

Rhiannon removes her hand, and there's the hollow sound of this particular tree cackling, so I know that heart or no heart, being let go is not an option.

"You mean I'll never get away from this tree," I say. "I'll never get out of this forest." My voice is thick, like someone poured a bottle of maple syrup down my throat, and I almost choke on the next words: "I'll never get to Quinn."

Rhiannon doesn't even seem to feel bad for me. She's very matter-of-fact about the whole thing. "We'll continue on without you and do our best to get your sister back in one piece."

"That's good, but . . . but you'll just leave me here–forever?"

"I'm afraid we have no choice."

"But if I'm stuck here, I won't have any food or water. I'll starve to death. Actually, I'll die of thirst first. Did you know that without water, you start dying in three days? That's why it's so important to keep yourself hydrated."

"Maybe it'll rain, and you can open your mouth and drink," Rafael says. I know he's trying to give me hope, but it doesn't make me feel any better. Even if it does rain within three days, and I'm saved, it needs to keep raining every three days to keep me living. Besides, what kind of life will it be, being trapped in a tree with only raindrops to swallow? Without food, I'll die of starvation in three weeks, anyway. And I won't have any company, except for the tree that is imprisoning me in the first place.

I shake my head, my hair tangling in the twigs and leaves. "Maybe dying of thirst quickly would be better," I say.

"Let's get going," Rhiannon tells Athena and Rafael. "We still have work to do."

They both look sad. In fact, Rafael looks like he's trying not to cry. But still, they leave me. As they're walking off, heads down, shoulders slumped, Rafael steps over the same root I tripped over. "TAKE THAT, YOU STUPID

TREE!" he yells.

"Rafael!" Rhiannon cries. "Do not do not DO NOT touch the roots of the tree!"

But it's too late. The tree lets out a deep groan, and Rhiannon yells to Rafael: "RUN FOR IT!"

Rafael is startled for a second, so he doesn't take off right away, and that's too bad because in that split second, a tree branch swoops down and plucks him up from the ground. I twist my head to the side and watch what happens through the leaves. It reminds me of the metal hand in one of those arcade machines. The kind with all the plush toys inside a big glass case. You put in a dollar and then you steer the metal hand to grab a toy. When Quinn and I were little, we always wanted to play that game. Dad would give us each a dollar, and we'd try to win, and sometimes we'd get really close. The metal hand would pick up a toy, and we'd steer it toward the chute. But it always dropped back into the pile with the other toys, and we'd lose. Then we'd ask for more and more dollars, until Dad had spent ten bucks and we still didn't have any prizes.

Well, I'll tell you something: If this tree were playing that game, it would definitely win. Because even though Rafael is twisting and jerking and contorting his body every which way, the branch still has him in its clutches. Now Rafi is dangling high above the ground, and the tree is cackling harder than ever.

"Stupid tree," Rafael says again, but not as forcefully as the last time. You can tell he's really scared because his voice is shaky. I think he was sad and mad about me before, but the idea of being trapped in a titanium—no, sorry, barkanium—tree for the rest of his life, without food and only rain for water, has him terrified.

As for Athena, she's run (carefully, jumping over every root) at least fifty yards away from us. There are trees everywhere. This is a forest, after all, and she's crouched down on the mossy ground, shaking in fear. "Rhiannon? Where are you?" she calls.

That's a good question. Where is Rhiannon? I haven't seen her since the tree grabbed Rafael. I turn my head to look in the other direction, and that's hard to do, because at this point the branches are so tight around me, it's hard to move at all or even breathe. Every time I do move, they get tighter, and I'm afraid if they squeeze me any more, they'll squeeze me to death. That would probably be worse than dying from hunger and thirst.

"Zack!" Rafael calls from above me. "Zack, what are we going to do?"

"I don't know," I choke out. I've been so careful to avoid disastrous situations. I've been putting safety first all year. "I don't know how someone like me ended up in a situation like this," I say.

"Someone like you," a voice intones. It's a voice as deep as a cavern, and it sounds like it's coming from somewhere dark and far away.

I know it's the tree speaking. "Someone like you?" it repeats. "You mean a no-good, sniveling, careless little ingrate who knocks into another person's roots."

It doesn't seem the right time to point out that a tree isn't exactly *another* person.

"I'm sorry about that. Truly. I didn't mean to do it," is what I say.

"And I admit that I stepped on your root on purpose, but only because I knew my friend Zack didn't mean it and you wouldn't let him go," Rafael adds.

"Please, please, find it in your heart to let us go," I say. "We'll never step on one of your roots again."

"We'll never step on any tree's roots ever again!" Rafael cries.

"That's right," I agree. "We promise."

There's a pause, and for a second I allow myself to hope that the tree will listen to our pleas and let us go. But then there's a deep groan, the kind of groan that never means good news. "You're ingrates, the both of you," the tree says, its voice as deep as thunder.

Rafael and I are now both saying, "Please, please, we'll do anything." But the tree has shuddered into silence. Out in the forest, Athena is still crying for Rhiannon. Oliver-David is above us, flitting and buzzing about. How lucky to be something so small. Bugs don't have to worry about anything. They can fly high, away from trees that might grab them. And even if a tree did happen to grab Oliver-David, I bet he'd be small enough to fly right through the grip of its branches.

Lucky, lucky Oliver-David. I don't think he even cares about what's happening to Rafael and me. I crane my neck to see him flying. He's farting out little sparkles that spell *Linx* in cursive, over and over again.

And where is Rhiannon in all of this? She's the grown-up. She's supposed to protect us, like the chaperone of a field trip. This isn't like any field trip I've ever been on before. But still, she's practically abandoned us. Out of the corner of my eye I spot her, tiptoeing along the forest floor, occasionally bending to pick something up in her hands. Then she puts it down and picks something up again. I squint, wishing for genie vision. But I can't tell what she picked up and stuck in her pocket. Something small, the size of a stray bird feather.

Rhiannon takes her time walking back over to us to say good-bye, careful not to step on any roots as she goes. She passes by Athena. I hear Athena tell her, "Let's get out of here now, please. Before anything worse happens!"

What could be worse than Rafael and me trapped for life? I guess if you're Athena, it would be being trapped, too.

Rhiannon approaches us. "Well, boys," she says. "I'm sure you wish you could continue on as my students, but you've made some mistakes today, and mistakes have consequences."

"They certainly do," the deep voice of the tree intones.

"I'm not sure if I'll see the two of you again," Rhiannon continues. "Probably not."

I give an involuntary gulp. Rhiannon and I aren't exactly best friends. Still, it's weird for a teacher to tell you she'll never see you again.

"So let me give you a piece of advice before Athena, Oliver-David, and I get on our way," she says as she reaches into her pocket. There's something in her hand now, and she whips it out, holding it as high as she can. I can see what she's holding now. It *is* a feather. She rubs it along the bark, and a rumble begins from deep in the roots of the tree. The whole thing is shaking now, and there's the sound of deep laughter again. The branches that have been clutching Rafael and me so tightly suddenly uncoil. "Don't step on any roots!" Rhiannon cries. "JUST RUN!"

18

SENSE OF DIRECTION

"You didn't really think I'd leave you, did you?" Rhiannon asks Rafael and me. From the tone of her voice, it sounds like she thinks we were being ridiculous for worrying at all.

We're still in the forest, a safe distance from the clutches of that awful tree, and we're walking-not-running through it, being oh-so-careful not to step anywhere we shouldn't. We avoid all roots, twigs, and even old leaves that have fallen from the trees to the ground, because who knows; dead leaves could have feelings, too. Which means we're not exactly walking a straight line to the left, where I *felt* Quinn. But Rhiannon said that even with our stepping around everything, Oliver-David could keep us moving in the right direction. She said bats have a really keen sense of these things.

"You didn't answer my question," Rhiannon says. "Did you two really think I'd leave you high and dry in a tree?"

"Not so dry," Oliver-David buzzes from above. "Not dry at all. There's a mist. There's a fog. There is moisture in the air. They'd certainly get a bit watery, wet, and wilted."

Rhiannon gives an eye roll. "It's just an expression," she says.

I shrug at her, feeling sheepish. Actually, I'm feeling a mix of sheepish and relieved and not really believing anything that just happened. It all seems like a dream, or more like a nightmare. And I'm too twisted up inside to even invent a word that means all those things.

"Well, you fooled me," Rafael says. "I really

thought you were leaving us."

"Me too," says Athena. "I mean, I thought we were leaving them together." She looks over at Rafi and me, blushing, I think, with equal parts of embarrassment and shame. "I'm sorry, guys," she tells us.

We both mumble, "It's okay," even though I'm pretty sure neither one of us means it.

"Well, as long as I'm alive, I'd never leave any students behind," Rhiannon says. "And even if I wanted to, I couldn't."

"Your genie powers wouldn't let you leave us?" Rafael asks. "But we don't have genie powers in here."

"It's a violation of Genie Board Decision two thousand and four," Rhiannon explains. "No leaving sparkies behind in foreign parallels. I'd certainly be punished if I did so."

I nod. I don't really have anything to say. So Rhiannon rescued us from the tree–so what? We still haven't reached Quinn and rescued *her*, which is the whole point of being here in the thirteenth parallel. I'm back to thinking about my sister.

At the same time, I'm also concentrating on not stepping on anything I shouldn't. There can't be any more accidents between here and wherever Quinn is. We need to get to her—and it's taking a really long time. This forest is enormous. I can't see the end of it. We've been walking for so long that my legs are aching. It feels like weeks have passed since we've been here, or maybe a month. At the rate we're going, I'll probably reach my eleventh birthday before I reach my sister. And what will happen to Mom while she's waiting for us? Does this count as genie business, so she won't remember we exist? Or will she think we've been kidnapped and call the police? Maybe they're at my house on Earth right now. Maybe there's a search party looking for us. I wonder if Uncle Max is back from his own genie business. Does he know where we are?

Or maybe time here in the thirteenth parallel is relative, like in the fifth parallel. Maybe it's even slower here. I decide to ask Rhiannon: "How does time move here compared to on Earth?"

"Time is irrelevant in the thirteenth parallel," Rhiannon says. "That's part of what makes Linx's banishment here so tough to take. You could be here a day or a thousand years. It all feels the same."

"Oh," I say, not understanding at all. It doesn't matter, anyway. We'll be here as long as it takes to get to Quinn, and we keep walking.

"Hey, look at that tree root," Rafael says, pointing a few yards in the distance. "Doesn't that look a lot like the scuff mark I left when I stomped on the tree that was holding Zack? Do you think someone else stomped on a tree, too?"

"Maybe," I say.

"Probably not," Athena says. "Trees are trees. Sometimes they're thick, sometimes they're thin. Sometimes they have marks on them. Sometimes they don't. We've seen every kind of tree in this forest. I can't wait till we're in a place without them!"

"Yeah, I know what you mean," Rafael says. "I live in Brazil, and we have dense jungles that are beautiful to look at. But right now I'd love to see some sidewalks and buildings and concrete walls. I'm feeling swallowed up by nature right now. In fact, that tree is giving me flashbacks to when the other one tried to swallow me for real."

"It didn't try to swallow you," Athena says.

"What do you know?" Rafael asks. "You ran so far away, you wouldn't have seen if that tree squirted me with ketchup and put me in a hot dog bun."

Athena blushes uncomfortably.

"It's okay," I tell her. "I wouldn't have wanted to be that close to the tree, either. It is weird how this one looks the same."

"And one I saw a while back," Athena says. "It looked the same, too."

"Enough about that old tree," Oliver-David interrupts. "I heard a great joke. Do you know what the flower said to the canary?"

"No, what?" I ask.

But Rhiannon waves her hand to shush Oliver-David before he can respond. She's stopped walking, and she's looking right at the tree. Specifically at the tree root. Her eyes squint, and then they widen again. She turns to Athena, Rafael, and me and looks us up and down. She's got a frown on her face, and I'm worried that we're in trouble. But it turns out she's not mad at us.

"OLIVER-DAVID!" she screams out.

"Yes, Madam Rhiannon?" he replies.

I can tell he's trying to make his voice sound innocent, and I can tell he doesn't really feel innocent at all.

I can also tell, even before Rhiannon speaks another word, why she's mad at Oliver-David.

"Oh no!" I cry out. "It's not true. It can't be."

"What?" Athena says.

Rhiannon is shaking her head. "I'm afraid it is true," she says.

"What?" Now Rafael is asking.

"The tree," I say. "It's the same tree. We've been walking in circles this whole time. We're no closer to Quinn than we were when we started." I turn to Rhiannon. "That's it, right?"

"That's it," she says.

"It's okay, Zack," Rafael says. "Time is irrelevant, and we'll just keep going."

"But you're so tired, and I'm so tired, and Quinn . . ." My voice trails off. Without thinking, I let myself sink to the ground.

Above me, Rhiannon is glaring at Oliver-David. "What is wrong with you?" she asks. "Did your brain short-circuit or something?"

Oliver-David is looking back at her, his tiny little mouth curling into a tiny little smile on his tiny little face.

"Oh, you think this is funny, young man, do you?" Rhiannon says.

"No, I don't," Oliver-David says quickly. "Of course not. No way. Not at all."

"Then why are you smiling?"

He floats a little up and down again, the bumblebee equivalent to a shrug. "I'm nervous, I guess," he says. "Understandable, right?"

Rhiannon isn't having it. "Wipe that grin off your face," she tells him, and right away his expression changes from an amused one to a grim one. I almost feel sorry for him, but it's my sister who is being held by Linx, and it's Oliver-David's fault that we haven't rescued her yet. So I'm too mad to feel bad for him at all.

"I'm sorry, miss, ma'am, Your Majesty," he says. "The thirteenth parallel has so many twists and turns, especially in this forest. I got disoriented. I made a misstep, a miscalculation, a mistake."

"You bet you did," Rhiannon agrees. "A mistake of gigantic proportions that wasn't funny at all."

"Is it too late now to get to Quinn?" Rafael

asks her.

"Of course not," Rhiannon says. "We just need to move forward. Perhaps without Oliver-David."

And with that, she raises her hand.

"NOOOOOOO!" Oliver-David cries out. "Please. Don't flick me, don't banish me, don't send me away!"

Rhiannon holds her hand still. "All right," she says. "But you can do better–you must do better."

"I will."

When she lowers her hand, she grips my shoulder. "Let me help you up, Zack."

I shake my head. "I'm too tired. Time is irrelevant, and I think I'll just stay here forever."

"No, you won't," she says. Her voice is forceful. I know she's a teacher, and I'm the kind of kid who always listens to his teachers. Except right now. My limbs are too heavy. They're sinking into the ground. It's like my body is becoming a part of the forest floor.

"If you want to go on, go without me." I move from a sitting position to a lying-down one.

"Rafael, Athena," Rhiannon says. "It's up to us."

I assume that means that they're moving on without me, and I let my eyelids close. They're feeling even heavier than my arms and legs, like they've gained a thousand pounds–each! Two thousand pounds over my eyes. It feels good to close them.

But then I feel their hands on me. Rhiannon's hands and Rafael's and Athena's. Even Oliver-David's. He doesn't have hands, but he's pulling at the strands of hair on my head with his itty-bitty toes. I don't want to move. I'm so tired. I want to give up. I don't want to be anyone's brother. I don't have to save anyone. But they're tugging and pulling, harder and harder and harder, until it becomes too hard to stay on the ground. It's taking more energy *not* to stand up.

So I get up like they want me to. I'm about to say: *Fine, you got me up. But good luck getting me to walk anywhere.* The words are on the tip of my tongue. But now that I'm standing, I don't feel tired anymore. "Wow," I say. "It's the weirdest thing. When I was lying on the forest floor, my body felt so heavy, I thought there was no way I'd be able to take one step, let alone all the steps it'll take to get to Quinn. But now that I'm standing again, I really think I can. How did that happen? How did the feelings in my body change so fast?"

"That's the way this forest works," Rhiannon says. "If you sit down, it'll keep you down. But if you manage to pull yourself back up, then it won't be able to stop you from moving forward. When you're up, you're up, and now that you are, we can keep going."

So we keep going. Oliver-David leads us, but not in circles this time. I know because I've started feeling Quinn again. I can feel us getting closer and closer to her as we walk on and on and on. Skipping over roots and ducking under branches, and time is passing or not passing or whatever it does in the thirteenth parallel.

Finally, we're at the end of the forest. And the way you can tell we're at the end is there's a wall. It stretches up so high into the sky, it's like it's reaching for distant galaxies.

Athena puts out a hand and knocks on it. "Feels like concrete," she says.

"It is concrete," Rhiannon tells her. "Strongest stuff of its kind."

"Like barkanium?"

"Something like that," Rhiannon says. She looks up at Oliver-David. "Go and see if there's a break in the wall."

Before he can respond, she's sent him off with a flick, and he tumbles away.

When he flies back to us, he says, "No way, no how, no clue as to how to get around it."

"Very well," Rhiannon says.

"So now what?" asks Rafael.

"Now, Rafael," Rhiannon tells him gravely, "it is up to you."

19

A Swim in a Thousand Oceans

Rafael? What can he do about a concrete wall?

He's wondering the same thing, too: "What can I do?" he asks. "I'm no match for concrete—at least not without genie magic."

"You have your power," she tells him.

"Oh yeah." He steps forward and presses his palms to the wall.

Athena moves to touch the wall too, but Rhiannon pulls her back. "No!" she says sharply. "You'll interrupt the flow."

Interrupt the flow? What is she talking about?

Rafael's eyes are closed, and he's got his

hands pressed so hard against the wall, it's almost like they're sinking into it.

Wait a second, they *are* sinking into it. His hands are disappearing INSIDE THE WALL, and as it happens, the concrete starts rippling like waves. It's getting softer, and soon water begins to cascade, from all the way up in the sky down to the ground where we're standing. The wall has become a waterfall. You'd think it would wash us away, but no: it flows around us, in circles and squiggles, making rivers that extend forever and ever.

The light hits the water in a million different places, and there are rainbows everywhere. For a second I forget how frightened I am to be here in the thirteenth parallel, and how worried I am about Quinn. I stand there, staring at the water and the rainbows like I'm under a spell. I could stare at them forever. Not like thinking I could be on the forest floor forever because there was no reason to go on. This is a feeling of wonder, and I

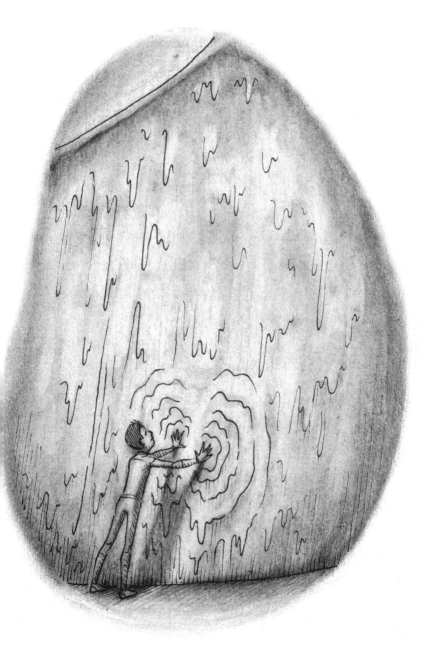

never want it to stop.

When Rafael finally steps away, a body of water stretches out in front of us. As big as the wall it replaced. "Whoa," Athena says. "Is that an ocean?"

"It's a thousand oceans," Rhiannon tells her. "But thanks to Rafael, now we can cross it."

"How?" I ask. "Our genie magic is gone."

And so is my feeling of wonder, replaced by a feeling of dread. Because I'm afraid I already know the answer.

And I do: "By swimming," Rhiannon says.

"No one can swim that far," I say. "We'll all drown."

"It's Rafael's power," Rhiannon says. "He'll keep us afloat."

Speaking of Rafael, he's already stepped into the water, Athena right next to him. They lift their arms above their heads and dive under. "Come on, Zack!" Rafael says. "Don't be afraid. It feels great."

Sometimes it amazes me how other people

can just do things without being scared. Is it because they don't know the danger? Or is there something in their brains that just makes them braver, something that is missing from my own brain?

I dip a foot into the water. A shiver runs from the tip of my big toe up through my body, and it's not because the water is cold. This ocean feels more like a bathtub–if there was ever a bathtub the size of the whole entire world. I quickly pull my foot out and look up at Oliver-David. I'm getting jealous of him again. Oh, to be a bumblebee bat. Or to be anything that flies. All he has to do is soar through the air to the other side.

"Let's get going, Zack," Rhiannon says.

"I can't," I tell her. "I know Rafael will help me. And more than that, I know we need to get to Quinn, but . . ." My voice trails off, and I stare into the distance of the unending water. "I can't do it."

"Of course you can," Rafael says.

"No, I–"

Rafael has raised a hand, and he puts it on my shoulder. The instant his fingertips touch me, tingles race through my body, from the tips of my toes to the top of my head. I know this feeling–the feeling of being shrunk down to fit inside of a genie bottle.

But that's not what's happening this time. My hands and legs and face and everything else aren't getting smaller. They're disappearing completely. In their place I grow some fins along my body and whiskers on the sides of my mouth.

"What's happening?" I try to say. My mouth opens and closes, opens and closes. It makes teeny little popping sounds, but no words come out.

"Whoa!" Rafael cries.

"You're a catfish," Rhiannon says. "Good work, Raf."

"I didn't know I was doing anything."

"Apparently your water powers are

transformative," she says. "You're not afraid of the water now, are you, Zack?"

I can't speak. I'm flapping in the sand, gasping for air through my . . . my gills!

But Rhiannon is right. I'm not afraid of the water. In fact, at this moment the only thing I want to do is get into it. That's easier said than done, since I don't have legs to carry me into the ocean. I flop and flop my body. I'm panting through my gills. This is so hard. Flop. Flop. Flop. My fish heart is beating hard. Rhiannon picks me up, and I try not to squirm in her grip, but I can't help it. "Stop that," she says. "I'm trying to help you."

And with that, she draws her arm back, like she's pitching a baseball, and throws me into the water.

SPLASH! Everything inside me calms down all at once. It's like being somewhere I've always belonged. Of course I belong here. I'm a fish, after all! Ha ha ha! I feel like laughing, and I would, if only I had a voice box. Instead my fins are flipping back and forth. I swim up to Athena and Rafael, and then I swim right past them. I feel like I could swim forever, and maybe I will. After all, isn't that what fish do? They swim, and they never stop. They swim even when they're going to the bathroom!

Not that I have to do that right now. I don't have to do anything but swim, swim, swim. I keep going. There in the distance is an enormous school of fish. I wonder if they're catfish, like me. Right now they look like little silver pinpricks, about a thousand of them.

They're getting closer. Hmm. What if they're not catfish? They could be predatory fish that would want to eat me. Largemouth bass, smallmouth bass, perch, walleye, striped bass, and pike, just to name a few. If any of those fish up there are those kind of fish . . . well, let's just say my plan for today does not include ending up as anyone's lunch.

I circle back toward Rhiannon, Rafael, and Athena. The other fish are getting closer.

Hang on.

It's not a school of fish.

It's about a thousand knives, shooting through the ocean toward us as fast as comets.

Holy smokes! I'm about to be a fileted fish!

The water is getting rougher with the force of the knives headed our way. "What do we do?" I hear Athena scream from above.

"Rafael, you had magic before," Rhiannon says. "Try it again!"

Rafael is snapping and pointing, but the knives are not stopping or slowing or changing direction. They're headed for us, and it's like a game of dodgeball. I'm playing for my life! It's a game I'm certain I'm going to lose. The knives are coming like bullets. Rhiannon and Rafael are treading water, trying to keep their legs as close to the surface as possible while still staying afloat. I dive down toward the ocean floor.

Meanwhile, Athena . . .

Oh no, Athena! The knives! They're all

headed toward her!

I'm watching in horror from the ocean floor. I want to cry out for her, but of course I'm a fish and I have no voice. They seem to strike her all at once, and I squeeze my eyes shut tight. I can't bear to watch.

Whoosh! Whoosh!

The water gets rougher as the knives strike. And then, suddenly, it's calm. I know Athena must be dead. Poor Athena. She only came here to help me save my sister, and now she's lying lifeless on the ocean floor.

I'm afraid of the blood, but I open my eyes a slit.

There lies Athena. And the knives.

She's not dead. She's not even bleeding. The tippy-tips of the knives are stuck to her, all over her body. Not piercing her. More like the points are attached with glue. And even though they're covering her from head to toe, I can tell she's completely unhurt.

I let out the breath I was holding through my gills, and the water ripples around me. Of course I want to ask how she's doing what she's doing. How did she stop all the knives, without a scratch on her? I open and close my mouth, open and close my mouth. No words, just bubbles.

Gingerly Athena kicks her legs and floats up to the surface. I follow, breathing shakily through my gills. Poor Athena doesn't have gills, and when she reaches the surface, she gasps for breath.

"I thought I was going to suffocate!" she cries.

"I thought the knives would kill you," Rafael says.

Oliver-David buzzes overhead. "Dead, deceased, departed, that's what I thought."

Rhiannon shakes her head: "Your superpower," she tells Athena. "You're a magnet. Just snap, and I bet the knives drop off your body and sink to the ground."

Athena does, and they do. She begins swimming forward again. So do the rest of us.

Time doesn't exist, and I can't tell you how long it is before we get to the other side of the ocean, but we get there eventually. Rhiannon, Rafael, and Athena walk right on out. Of course it's not as easy for me. I swim in a fast circle and leap up.

YOW!

Something big and furry just grabbed me.

Holy smokes! It's that two-headed grizzly bear again! How did it get here faster than we did?

Oh, who cares how it got here? All that matters is that I'm trapped in its enormous furry paw, the one it's lifting toward one of its smelly, saliva-filled mouths.

I want to shout: *Don't eat me! I'm the same kid as before!*

But of course all I can do is open and close my mouth, open and close my mouth. I'm about to be someone's lunch after all! I feel its hot breath on my gills and the tips of its enormous incisors about to pierce my scaly skin. And then–

SNAP!

My body tingles, and in an instant, I change from a catfish back to a ten-year-old boy. All of a sudden I'm too big for the bear's mouth, and it chokes me out. I land with a thud. I'm still wet from the ocean, plus the slime from the bear's mouth, and the sand sticks all over my body. Usually I hate feeling sandy, but that's the least of my problems.

"Sorry," the bear grumbles. It extends a bear paw again, and this time I let it help me to my feet. After all, it's now had several opportunities to eat me, and it has decided not to every single time.

"Thanks," I say.

The bear dives into the water, and the four of us walk up the dunes. Oliver-David flies nervously alongside. The sandy ground thins until it's nothing but dust, and it feels like there isn't anything under our feet, that we're just walking through space. A fortress materializes, with a big wooden door. Above it are gold letters, each as big as a mountain, spelling out the word LINX. They sparkle and blink in some kind of Morse code that seems to spell out *danger*.

"Is this where he lives?" Rafael asks.

"Yes," I say. Without really knowing it, I know it. I can feel the ache in my chest as strong as ever. I know he's in there, and I know Quinn is with him.

"Let's find our way in," Rhiannon says.

20

A Wish at the Door

Getting into Linx's fortress isn't like getting into anyone else's house. There's no doorbell or door knocker. There's not even a doorknob. Rhiannon sends Oliver-David around, like she did when we came upon the wall, to see if there's an easy way in. But he comes back and reports: "Zip, zilch, nothing."

"Are you sure?" she asks.

"Well, there were some marks on a wall in the back," he says. "They looked like fingerprints. Nothing significant."

"Oliver-David, you are a bumblebee bat,"

Rhiannon tells him sternly. "What do you know of significance?"

"As a matter of fact, I know a lot of things," Oliver-David begins. "I know–"

"I believe I'll be the judge of what is and isn't significant," Rhiannon says, cutting him off. She turns to Athena, Rafael, and me. "Come along, sparkies."

We walk under a starless sky to the side of the building. Once again, everything is dark. But we do have the light from the blinking L-I-N-X light, and I can see what Oliver-David was talking about–the residue of fingerprints on a back wall. They have a fluorescent glow to them, as if someone colored a finger with a highlighter pen, then pressed it down. I push my own hand against it, right where the fingerprint is, and a shock flies out, like a mini strike of lightning. "Ouch!" I cry, falling backward, right into Rafael.

"Oof!"

"Sorry."

"Don't use your hand," Rhiannon says.

Now she tells me.

"Those aren't fingerprints," she goes on. "Those are toe prints. From genie-bitten toes. Those are the only things that leave that kind of mark. Right shoes off, everyone."

"We're going to climb the wall?" Athena asks. "Barefoot?!"

"Of course not," Rhiannon says. "It's just your right shoe. Now off with it. I believe we are dealing with a toe lock, which means our toe prints will unlock the door."

"The door? What door?"

"I have a feeling we're about to find out."

Athena kicks her right shoe off, and so do the rest of us. Our genie bites all have a fluorescent glow. I stare at my own greenish-yellow squiggle and dot.

Rhiannon goes first, pressing her right big toe into the toe-print indentation. "I barely felt it," she reports. "Now you, Athena."

Athena cringes, but she does the same. Then Rafael, and then it's my turn.

I wish this works. I wish this works. I wish this works, I'm thinking. My toe is tingling as I put it in the exact same spot; when I do, I feel something right on my genie bite. A shock again, but not a big one. Like I was just hit by the world's smallest bolt of lightning. That's it.

"Will the door open?" I ask.

"No," Rhiannon says. "And I should've known."

"What? Why?"

"The rules of a toe lock," she says. "The eldest among us–that's me, in case you're counting years here–the eldest among us hails from the fifth parallel, so we need a quintet of footprints to open that door."

"And since Moe left, we're a quartet," Athena says.

"Exactly."

"So we came all this way for nothing?"

230

Oliver-David asks. He's got that little smile back on his face. Maybe it's a nervous kind of smile; but nerves or not, this is no time for smiles.

I turn away from Oliver-David so I don't have to look at him. "It can't be for nothing!" I cry out.

"No, it's not for nothing," Rhiannon agrees. "I just need to think of what to try next."

"My uncle would know," I say. "Do you think he's back from genie assignment yet?"

Before she answers, I have my toe pinched between my fingers. That's the genie way of calling. You need a bottle too, and I don't have mine. But Rhiannon has hers, and I'm hoping Uncle Max's head will appear like a hologram, the way it did when I was off on genie assignment in Grovestand, California, and I'd accidentally turned Trey into Quinn and Linx had appeared.

I'm squeezing my toe as hard as I can and wishing desperately for help to arrive. Uncle Max's head doesn't appear.

But something else is happening. The bottle hanging around Rhiannon's neck has suddenly started to glow fluorescent yellow, like the mark of a genie toe print. Now it's blue, now it's pink, and now it's the greenest green there ever was.

"What's happening?" Athena asks.

"I think we're about to get our answer," Rhiannon says, and an itty-bitty Moe pops out.

Pop! Pop! Pop!

His limbs and appendages and face and torso all pop back to their regular sizes.

"Welcome back," Rhiannon says, smoothing her necklace back around her neck. "I'm glad you're with us again."

"Me too," Rafael says.

"Me three," says Athena.

"And especially me," I say.

"I can fill you in on what you've missed because I've taken notes on it all," Oliver-David says. He reaches into a pocket in his wing and pulls out a scroll. "Let's see, first we were chased by wild animals."

"He was there for that," Athena says. "That's why he left us."

"Sorry," Moe says sheepishly. "I'm back now. I'm not sure how it happened. But here I am."

"I wished it," I say. "I didn't know genie wishes could come true. But I wished for help, and right away, you appeared, and–"

"Ahem," Oliver-David interrupts. "As I was saying. Then we entered a forest, and Zack and Rafael got caught in the trees."

"More like they caught us," Rafael says.

"Potay-to, potah-to," Oliver-David says. "This is my list, and I'll read it my way. We came upon a cement wall, stronger than barkanium, but Rafael turned it into water–a little too much water, if you ask me."

"No one asked you," Rafi mutters.

"Then there were knife-shaped fish."

"That was my genie superpower," Athena says. "They all stuck to me like magnets, and I saved everyone."

"Right, so now here we are," says Oliver-David. "Oh, and Zack almost got eaten by a bear again."

"I haven't figured out my genie superpower yet," I say. "But it's sure not avoiding bears."

"Let's leave the bears out of this," Rhiannon says. "The important thing is we have Moe back with us, so we have our fifth genie toe print. And that, my friends, is Moe's superpower."

"It is?" Rafael asks. "I thought any genie toe print would do."

"Indeed it would. But Moe's superpower is being here, at the exact time when he was needed."

"How is that a power?" Moe asks.

"You can sense when your friends need you, and you appear. Ask anyone who has ever needed a friend: That is a superpower."

I look at Moe. "It sure is."

"Now," says Rhiannon. "Put your toe here."

Moe does what the rest of us have done: He puts his toe print right on the fluorescent marks. There's a deep rumble. I've never been in an earthquake before, but I'm pretty sure it would sound like this, like everything is crumbling away. There are cracks appearing in the wall, and then a door shape, and then it opens. Beyond it is a flicker of light coming through clouds of smoke. We're all shivering in fear, but we step forward. It's the only thing to do. We can barely see each other as we walk, that's how thick the smoke is. But we form a chain, all holding hands. I'm next to Rhiannon. Oliver-David is perched on her shoulder, and I can feel him shaking next to me.

"Rhiannon?" I ask.

"Yes."

"How come my wish for Moe came true? None of the other wishes I've ever wished have come true, up till now."

"I think there's a force greater than the rest of us in charge right now, deciding what to grant and not grant," Rhiannon says.

"Right you are," a deep voice intones.

I know who it is.

It's Linx.

21

It's Quinn and I'm Dreaming

I'm having the strangest dream, and I can't wake up from it. But that's fine; I don't want to. Dreams are kind of nice, sometimes. You get a break from the things in your life that you wish you could change but you can't. And there are plenty of things that I wish I could change.

Like my dad. In real life he's gone, but in this dream he is back. He's back, and he's making pancakes for breakfast again. Pancakes for breakfast by my chef-dad, like everything is normal, or maybe even better than normal. This is the best breakfast a girl could wish for. My dad lets me drop the chocolate chips into the batter. A quarter of the bag, half the bag, the whole bag. "These are going to be the chocolatiest pancakes in the universe!" he says.

"Cool! Can I invite my friends?"

"No!" Dad says.

"No?"

"No, it's just us, darling."

"What about Zack?"

"Do you really want your brother in here?"

I think about that. Hmm. Probably not. I wish I had a normal brother, but Zack is anything but normal. If he were here, he'd be doing his weird Zack-things, like checking a dozen times to make sure all the burners on the stove are turned off. Or testing the batteries in the smoke detector out in the hall and making sure our fire extinguisher is in working order. No, no, I don't need him here.

Dad sits down beside me at the island in the kitchen and serves our pancakes. They're in different letter shapes. I look for a *Q* to eat first, but there isn't one. Instead, the letters on my plate are *L-I-N-X*. That's not normal.

"Dad?" I say.

But when he looks up at me, it's not Dad at all. It's someone else. Someone bigger and redder. I've never seen anyone with red skin before.

I try to open my eyes to wake up, but they're already open.

This is not a dream. This is not even a nightmare. Nothing about my life is normal.

"You want normal, Quinn," the red monster says. "You must wish for it."

I wish . . .

22

AT LAST WE MEET AGAIN

The smoke has cleared, and there is Linx standing in front of us. He looks just like I remember–tall and broad, red skinned and red eyed, with hair thick and black as a starless sky.

It's hard to believe that this man is Uncle Max's brother–his *twin*. Uncle Max is taller than I am, but not by much. He's thin, with white hair and wrinkly skin that is especially bunched up around his eyes. His eyes make him look like he's smiling even when he's not. I know Quinn makes fun of him sometimes, but the truth is, Uncle Max looks like a nice old man. He looks the opposite of the man in front of me now.

I miss Uncle Max so much right now. Wherever he is, I wish he were here. But there's no time to get into all of that. "Give Quinn back," I say to Linx.

"Oh, come now, Zack," Linx says, his voice coming out smooth and even, like he's a good guy and this is just your run-of-the-mill social visit. "Is that any way to greet your uncle—your *real* uncle?"

He doesn't wait for me to answer. Instead, he cackles like he's just told the world's funniest joke. His body rocks, and the building shakes around us. We huddle together, and Linx brings a finger to his lips. His palms are as big as baseball mitts, and his fingers are as long and thick as sausages. He licks the tip of the meaty pointer finger on his right hand. I feel my breath catch in my throat. Magic is about to happen again—and not the good kind. The very, very bad kind.

I'm holding my body so stiff, waiting for something to explode, waiting for someone to disappear, waiting for the world to crumble around us. But nothing like that happens. The only thing that moves is Oliver-David. He flies off Rhiannon's shoulder and lands on Linx's outstretched hand.

"Oliver-David!" Rhiannon cries out. The poor bat is attached to Linx's finger like a magnet. Like those knives that got stuck to Athena. He has no choice.

"Let him go!" I say.

Linx cackles again, so deeply that the air around us seems to vibrate with the sound, and he shakes his head from side to side. "Tsk, tsk, tsk," he says. "I would've expected better manners from my *nephew*."

"*Please*," I say. "Please let him go. And Quinn, too, wherever she is."

"That's more like it," Linx says. "But there's something you should know about your friend Oliver-David here."

"What?" Rhiannon asks, and I can sense the

fear in her voice. What did Linx do to Oliver-David?

Linx lifts his right hand up so it's in front of his face, and he speaks to Oliver-David at eye level. "Do you want to tell them, or should I?"

"It's up to you, master," Oliver-David says.

Master?!

"Then allow me," Linx says. He reaches his left hand over and gently strokes Oliver-David's back with a finger. "This little guy doesn't work for you. He works for me."

"No, he doesn't," I say. "He belongs to Rhiannon."

"I belong to myself," Oliver-David interrupts.

"Zack means you *work* for me, Oliver-David," Rhiannon says.

"Of course," I say. "Of course that's what I meant. You live in the fifth parallel with her. And you came here to the thirteenth with us. Your sense of direction guided us here to Linx." I turn to the red genie. "He wouldn't have done that if he were working for you."

"Precisely," Rhiannon says. Moe, Athena, and Rafael nod in agreement.

"Oh, how adorable," Linx says, and he shares a little laugh with Oliver-David. "These so-called friends of yours are such adorable little fools." He turns back to us. "Do you think you'd be here if I didn't want you here?"

"You didn't want us here," I argue. "We had to travel for so long. For hundreds of miles, or maybe even thousands. I don't know how long it took."

"Time is irrelevant here."

"That's what Rhiannon said, but I swear the minutes were ticking by forever. And it wasn't just the time and distance. There were obstacles, too. We fought off wild animals, we hiked through a forest, we swam across an ocean."

"If you wanted us here, wouldn't it have been easier?" Athena adds.

Linx shakes his head, laughing again.

"Easy," he says, repeating the word as if it's a concept Athena just made up. "You couldn't have expected me to make it easy. But trust me, my little birdbrains, your being here is part of my plan. I led you here–with a little help from my friend."

"He means ME!" Oliver-David shouts with pride, and he shoots up from Linx's hand and lands back down again. I look at Rhiannon, whose face has turned stony, as expressionless as a statue.

"Why would you choose to work for him?" Moe asks incredulously.

"Because he is the strongest, the greatest, the most powerful genie in the universe. And he is going to help me get my name in lights. Isn't that right, Sir Linx?"

"Of course," Linx says.

"Oliver-David," Rhiannon says softly, "whatever he has told you, it's not true. You don't have to do this."

"But I want to do this," Oliver-David insists. "He's going to give me the life I've *always* wanted!"

And with that, Oliver-David flies up again and sparkle-farts out his name, dotting the *i*'s with stars.

Linx cackles some more. "Oliver-David, come here, please," he says, holding out his palm.

Oliver-David obliges. The instant he's settled on Linx's hand, Linx curls his fingers into a fist.

It happens so quickly.

There's a sharp *crunch* sound that sends a chill up my spine. Oliver-David doesn't so much as let out a whimper. And when Linx unfolds his hand, there's the bumblebee bat, lying crumpled on his palm. Rhiannon gasps, and Athena starts crying. Moe and I stand in shocked silence.

"He can't really be dead," Rafael says, his voice barely a whisper.

Linx wipes his palms of the remains of Oliver-David. His ruined little body falls to the floor. Rhiannon bends down and pets him. He looks even tinier now, just a collection of little broken bones. "Nothing but vermin," Linx says coldly.

"Can you save him?" Athena cries.

Rhiannon shakes her head. "We can't bring anyone back to life. Even if I had genie magic, I couldn't do that."

"You said you'd put his name in lights, and now look at him!" I shout. "You took advantage of his dearest wish! You're a monster!"

"I'm a genie," Linx tells me. "I will always grant wishes."

And right then, by Oliver-David's pathetic little carcass, something appears. It's a headstone, his name carved out in block letters. Linx wags a finger and the letters are illuminated.

"There you go," Linx says. "His name in lights. Will there be anything else?"

I'm afraid to ask about my sister. What wishes of hers will be distorted? What wishes of mine?

My heart is pounding with faster *humming-*

beats than ever before—like a gazillion humming-birds are in there, and they are all hyped up on sugar and caffeine. I know Quinn's life is on the line. I don't want her to end up crushed in Linx's fist. She's significantly bigger than Oliver-David; still, she is much smaller than Linx, and it is clear to me that he could crush her, too, without any feeling of remorse or shame.

"And as for your sister," Linx says, as if he's reading my mind—and who knows? Maybe he is. "She is here completely and totally of her own volition, too."

I shake my head. "I don't believe it. I really don't believe it."

"Unless you tricked her," Rafael adds.

Now it makes sense. He tricked her. Just like he tricked Oliver-David. Just like he almost tricked me back in Grovestand, California, when he told me he'd grant my dearest wish.

I wonder what Quinn's wish is. I wonder what Linx has promised her.

The fog is swirling about again, and everything has turned blurry, except for Linx. I can see him clearly. Rhiannon picks up the remains of Oliver-David and puts him gently in her pocket. I don't know what she plans to do with a dead bumblebee bat, and I don't get a chance to ask because the ground is shifting beneath us. I try to keep from falling, but it's no use. I stumble to the ground.

When the shaking stops and I look up again, everything is different. We're standing in clouds at the foot of a mountain. Linx is at the top. He's so big, it's impossible to miss him, no matter how far away he is. And there's something–or someone– next to him. Whatever, whoever it is, they barely come up to his knees. It's so hard to tell, but I think it's my sister.

In fact, I'm sure it's her. I can *feel* it.

"Quinn!" I call. "I'm coming for you!"

"Come on, kids," Rhiannon says to the others. "Let's go."

I've started up the mountain already, and they race to catch up. I feel Rafael's hand on my shoulder, and I pat it, a silent thank-you. I'm about to tell him that out loud. I'm about to say how much I need a best friend, and how grateful I am that he's here beside me. But just before the words leave my mouth, Rafael lifts his hand away.

No, he didn't lift it away. It was zapped back. Along with the rest of his body. He's falling down the mountain. Within seconds, he seems miles away. Same for Athena, Moe, and Rhiannon. I'm standing alone, and the only thing I can do is watch them, tumbling like laundry. I can hear them crying out in frustration or maybe even pain.

"What's happening?" I call.

But I already know the answer. When I look back up at Linx, he's laughing so hard, he's doubled over. But even bent in half, he's still the largest man I've ever seen.

"It's not funny!" I shout. "It's not funny at all!"

Linx takes a breath so deep, it's like he's sucking in all the oxygen in the world. The clouds sweep toward him as he inhales. They disappear up his nose and into his mouth. Then he breathes them out again.

"You're right," he says, now that he's composed himself. "That wasn't funny. But this will be."

He twirls his finger and points it at me. I squeeze my eyes shut and brace myself for a down-the-mountain tumble. How in the world will I get to Quinn now?!

Seconds pass. I don't feel anything happening. Then it's a minute, or two, or twelve. Who knows in this place where time doesn't exist? All I know is my feet still feel firmly planted on the ground. I open one eye a slit, then the other. Unless Linx has magically created some sort of illusion, it looks like I'm still standing on the mountain. It certainly seems real.

"Ha ha ha!" Linx cackles. "Psych!"

I shake my head. I keep going.

One foot in front of the other, and then the other, and then the other. Behind me I can hear cheers of my friends and Rhiannon, and then I'm too far away and I don't hear them at all.

This is the toughest hike of my life. It's like climbing Mount Everest, which I would never do. Do you know how many people have died trying to climb to the peak of Mount Everest? Two hundred and forty people. If you're putting safety first, you definitely wouldn't climb Mount Everest.

Those climbers had a choice. But I don't. I'm cold and wet and tired and I have to pee. Each step I take, the mountain seems to be growing. But finally I get to the top.

"Zachary," Linx says. "At last we meet again."

23

You Still Want a Dog?

Quinn and I aren't exactly huggy with each other on normal days. But there is nothing normal about this day, and as soon as I get to the top of the mountain, I make a move to throw my arms around her.

"Quinn!" I cry out.

But she stops me with a raised hand, and though she doesn't say anything, I know her hand is speaking for her. It's saying: *Don't you dare hug me, you nut job.* I guess she's mad at me. But what for? For leaving her at Uncle Max's? That was HER idea. Besides, I didn't know what would happen.

"I didn't know this would happen," I say. "You've got to believe that—"

"That's enough," Linx interrupts. "Now that you're here, we can get on with granting Quinn's dearest wish."

"Quinn's dearest wish?" I ask. "Now that I'm here?"

"I cannot grant the wish of one twin without the presence of the other," Linx explains.

"You're bluffing," I say. "I know you're bluffing. You said you could grant my wish when I was in California on genie assignment. You didn't need my twin there. Quinn, he's trying to trick you!"

"Ah," Linx says. "Clever boy. But what you're forgetting is that only *your* genie powers had emerged back then—not Quinn's. The rules have changed. It's a little kink in the system. One I'll certainly repair the moment this transaction is complete. Now, Quinn—"

"Don't say anything!" I tell my sister.

"You can't tell me what to say or not to say," she says.

"I'm sorry," I say. "I know I shouldn't have left you at Uncle Max's and gone to SFG without you."

"It's fine," she says coolly.

"You don't sound like you really think it's fine," I tell her.

"No, I mean it," she says. "I told you to leave me back at the house, and now it seems as though everything worked out for the best."

Worked out for the best?! Is she kidding me? She must be kidding me.

"This is no time for jokes," I say. I quickly glance up at Linx. He has an amused look on his face, like he thinks all of this is very funny. "Listen, I get that you're mad at me. I said I was sorry."

"I'm not mad," Quinn says.

"You're really not?"

"No, I'm really not," she says. "Now get a grip and stop being a nut job."

"I'm not a nut job; *you're* a nut job," I mutter.

Above us, Linx has started cackling. "Seeing the two of you," Linx says between bouts of laughter, "it's bringing back cherished childhood memories."

"How could you have cherished memories?" I ask. "Rhiannon said you had a bad childhood." I pause, thinking. Maybe what Linx really needs is an apology. Sure he's done a lot of awful things, but it all started because his brother gave him a hard time. "I want to tell you something on behalf of Uncle Max," I say.

"Your so-called uncle gave you a message for me?"

"Not exactly," I say. "But he did tell me it was important for genie twins to get along. I think he'd want me to tell you this."

"What?"

"I'm sorry."

"You?" Linx says, practically spitting the word out. "You're sorry for me?"

"I know what it's like to be a twin," I say. "I know it's hard sometimes. I know Uncle Max was mean to you. I wasn't there back then, but I think he probably just felt a little bit jealous."

"That's rich. Max jealous of *me*."

"Maybe," I say. "He didn't tell me for sure." I pause again, then add: "But I know that I'm jealous of my sister sometimes."

"You don't act jealous," Quinn cuts in. "You act like you don't care about anything in my life. You say that the things that are important to me are dumb—even though they're not dumb at all."

"Then I apologize to you, too, for that," I tell my sister. "Not on behalf of anyone else. Just on behalf of me. I *do* care about things in your life."

"Sure you do," Quinn says sarcastically, and Linx laughs again.

"I love seeing siblings go head-to-head," he says. "This is better than anything you'd see on television."

"We can talk about all of this just as soon as we're safe," I tell my sister.

"You're safe here, Quinn," Linx says.

"Quinn, come on," I say.

My sister turns to me. "If you're so sorry, then why do you make fun of my friends—and why don't you try to make friends of your own? That's a normal thing to do. This genie business is NOT normal."

"I can fix that for you, Quinn," Linx says.

"And if you want to have friends," my sister continues to me, softly, "you *have* to be normal."

"I have friends," I say. "I have Rafael. And Moe and Athena, too."

"Yeah, yeah. But they're not normal friends."

"Maybe they're even better," I tell her. "They came here with me, and they like you. At first that made me mad. I was . . . well, I was jealous, like I said before. I was finally popular somewhere, and I didn't want to have you come in and be more popular and ruin it for me. But I don't mind sharing them now. We can all be friends."

"I'm not interested in your genie friends," Quinn says. "I already had what I need, and Linx says I can have it again."

"That's right, Quinn," Linx says. "What's yours is yours, and what's Zack's is Zack's."

"Uncle Max says it isn't that way at all," I tell her.

"Ha!" Linx says. "Shows what he knows. He thought he could banish me and be done with it. Now look–I have his great-grandchildren to the seventh degree standing at my feet. Who's jealous of whom now?"

I'm trying to think of something to do, some distraction, so I can grab Quinn and run down the mountain to Rhiannon and the bottle. But before I can think up anything, Linx reads my mind again.

"If you and your sister want to leave me and go home, go on," he says. "I'm not going to stop you."

"You mean we can just leave?" I ask. "Right now?"

"Sure," he says. "Walk down the mountain. Or run down. Or skip. The crowd is waiting below."

I'm sure Linx is joking; but the thing is, he doesn't look like he's joking. "Come on, Quinn," I say.

"No," my sister tells me.

"But we can leave. He says so."

"I'm not going. I want my wish."

She looks over at Linx, and he gives her a nod as if to say, *Go ahead. Make your wish. Make it now.*

Quinn opens her mouth to speak.

"Noooooo," I say, the word stretching out, time unending. "Don't do it! If you do it, you'll never be able to take it back."

Quinn breaks her gaze from Linx and swivels her head toward me. "But I want to," she says. "I don't want to be a genie. I want to be normal.

He says he can take all the genie stuff away from me, and give me back my normal life–and that includes Dad! Because it's not normal to not have a dad anymore. You want him back, too, don't you?"

"Yeah, of course," I say. "But it's not going to work out the way you think it will. That's what Linx does. He tells you things he thinks you want to hear. Like he promised me a dog–he promised me two of them."

"I'd be happy to give you a dog, Zack," Linx says. "Just let your sister make her wish."

"It's a trick," I go on. "He wants your power for himself."

"My power?"

"Your GENIE powers."

"That's fine with me. I don't want them."

"Just give it a chance," I implore my sister. "You're good at being normal–better than I am. But you'll be good at this, too."

"Don't let your brother talk you out of what

you want," Linx says.

"I'm only trying to tell you that you're going to end up wanting this," I say. "You're good at making friends. That's your talent, and now it makes sense why this is your destiny."

"I don't get it," Quinn says. "I just want a life I understand again."

"Say the words," Linx says.

"When people tell you their wishes, they're telling you about themselves," I say. "They're trusting you. It's like you're their best friend for that moment."

"I want the friends I have right now," Quinn says, her voice thick. "My friends at school. I *miss* them."

"They're still there," I tell her. "They're right where you left them. It's about balance. Uncle Max told me, but I didn't understand until this second. We can go home right now, Quinn. There will be times when we need to be genies, but for now let's go home."

"Quinn," Linx says, "you don't have to listen to a word your brother says. You have words of your own."

"Okay," she says.

"Okay?" Linx and I both repeat, and then I hold my breath, worrying that the next words out of Quinn's mouth will be the dreaded *I wish* . . .

But instead, she turns to me. "Let's go home."

We move to step away, down the mountain, but Linx's voice is a roar louder than a thousand oceans, louder than every animal in the entire animal kingdom. "Not so fast!" he shouts.

"You said we could go if Quinn wanted to!" I cry.

"Never mind what I said," Linx growls. He swings a finger, and the ground starts to shake beneath us.

"EARTHQUAKE!" Quinn shrieks.

24

TEN THOUSAND AND TWO

Did you know that on average, ten thousand people die in earthquakes each year? It looks like there are about to be two more.

Quinn and I have both dropped to the ground. It's opened up beneath us, and I'm hanging on, trying not to fall through the cracks. But the ground keeps shaking, and the cracks widening.

"Stop it!" I scream at Linx. "Stop it right now!"

"Not until I get what I want," he says. "The power of a genie twin."

"Fine," I say. "You can take mine. You can have my power."

"Zack!" Quinn screams. But Linx stops her with a snap. Her mouth is sealed.

"Say the words," he says to me.

"I wish–" I begin.

I see Quinn pleading with me with her eyes. She's hanging on to the edge by the tips of her fingers, but at that moment, before the next word leaves my mouth, she grabs my hand.

Quinn never wants to hold my hand. But now she's squeezing it extra tight. And suddenly there's a light that is positively blinding. I have to shut my eyes. I squeeze Quinn's hand, too. I can't tell where my hand ends and hers begins. Something, some force, shoots us up from the cracks and onto solid ground. I can feel it under my feet. Everything feels stronger, and I realize something–this is my superpower. It's Quinn and me. Together, we are so strong. I think we may even be strong enough to defeat Linx.

"Zack, what's happening to us? Zack?" Quinn calls. I don't know the answer, but at least she can speak again.

"Genie?" another voice calls. A boy's voice. It's familiar, but I can't place it, and then . . .

"Trey, is that you?" I ask.

"Of course it's me," he says.

Holy smokes! It's Trey!

TREY! My genie assignment! All the way from Grovestand, California! What is he doing here?

"What's happening?" he cries. "Where am I? Why am I blind? What did you do to me, genie?!"

"I don't know," is all I can say.

"You remember who my father is," Trey says. "Preston Hudson Twendel the second. Owner of PHT Capital. When he hears about this, HE WILL EXPLODE!"

It's hard to worry about Trey's father's explosive personality, even if he owns the biggest bank in the world. It doesn't matter how powerful all his money makes him, because Linx's power is the kind that even money can't buy, and he's got us trapped here in the thirteenth parallel.

We're all screaming, and there's another sound, too, a sound like an animal. I open my eyes just a slit. It's Linx crying out. The light is doing something to him, lifting him up, contorting his body.

"Quinn, Trey!" I say. "We need to go! NOW!"

Quinn and I are still holding hands, and Trey grabs on to my arm. We run down the mountain. Running turns into somersaults, because they're faster, and we can't get to the bottom fast enough. We're like champion gymnasts, rolling over and over. I bet Simone Biles has never somersaulted so quickly in her life. Genie tumbling should be an Olympic sport.

Rhiannon and the others are at the bottom. Trey doesn't know who they are, obviously, but there aren't any introductions, just Rhiannon snapping around. Her bottle is glowing, and one by one she points to each of us and shrinks us down. Moe, Athena, Rafael, Trey, then Quinn and me. My body is tingling, shrinking, flying toward the opening of the bottle. My hands become mini-sized, as do Quinn's, and we're momentarily separated from each other.

But my ears are still working, and a voice from above intones, "Still want a dog, Zack? How about one you'll share with your sister? If you're so good at sharing now."

It's more like a growl than a voice, and in an instant, a giant red dog is down the mountain in two enormous strides.

I don't need anyone to tell me that the red dog is Linx. He's transformed himself. The top of the bottle is just inches away, and my sister and I are buzzing toward it. But before we reach it, he swallows us in a gulp.

The inside of Linx the Dog's mouth is dark and slimy. But I didn't escape a two-headed grizzly bear's mouth–twice–to end up as this creature's lunch.

It's impossible to get close enough to his

mouth to get out. He keeps chomping his teeth like he's trying to chew us up. Humans have a gag reflex, if food gets too close to the back of their throats without being chewed up small enough. The gag reflex is supposed to stop us from choking on pieces that are too big to swallow. I hope dogs have that reflex, too.

"Quinn," I say in my tiny shrunk-down voice. "Get as close to the front as you can. I'm going to tickle his throat, and you've got to be ready when he throws us up."

I'm tickling and tickling. It worked when Rhiannon tickled the barkanium. But it's not working now. I'm too small. The dog's throat is constricting and opening, constricting and opening. He's trying to swallow me, and if that happens, there won't be any hope at all. Not unless he poos me out, and I don't even want to think about that. I grab ahold of one of the back molars, hanging on with all my might.

I will not be swallowed. I will not be swallowed.

Quinn is whipped toward me by the force of Linx's dog tongue. We grab hands again. If we're going to die inside this dog, at least we'll die together.

We're at the base of Linx's tongue, kicking our legs with all our might, and suddenly there's a wind from the back of his throat, as forceful as a hurricane and as rank as a garbage dump.

But who cares about the smell. Linx the Dog is retching. Maybe I was too small on my own to tickle the back of his throat, but Quinn and I together have done it! His mouth opens to throw us up. We're covered in slime and bits of food, but we can see the bottle still there, glowing before us. Rhiannon and the others are gone. The glow of the bottle is fading, fading. One more second, and it would've been gone.

Linx growls. Quinn and I are sucked inside. Are we in a wormhole? Are we in Linx's doggie intestines? There's only one way to find out. I squeeze my sister's hand and hang on for the ride.

25

QUINN GETS THE LAST CHAPTER

I grant a wish from my first genie assignment, sort of.

It's Zack's genie assignment, but it's mine, too.

His name is Trey, and just a couple of weeks ago, Zack was summoned to his school in Grovestand, California. Trey wished to be someone who other people liked. But my nut job brother messed it up. I guess it wasn't really his fault. He was just a sparkie, after all. He turned Trey into me, because I am someone people like. I am popular. Which is a cool thing to be. But it's not the only thing that matters in my life. I learned that when I was almost killed a few times.

Anyway, in the end, Trey's wish ended up undoing itself, and no one knew why. It turned

out that reason was me.

We're a pair, my brother and I. We're genie twins, and like it or not, we're stuck with each other.

(To be honest, I do kind of like it. But don't tell my brother that.)

Once Zack and I are together, Trey's wish comes true. We don't see it, but we know. Rhiannon is about to snap Trey back home, and he says, "Hurry up, or Nick will report me missing."

"Nick? Who's Nick?" Zack asks.

"My roommate, Nick Marx," Trey says. "Duh."

But then his mouth is an O, and he's just as surprised as we are. "I have a roommate," he says. "Except he didn't want to be my roommate."

"Oh my goodness!" Zack says. "Your wish! I think it worked! I think it redid itself!"

"People like me now?" he asks incredulously.

"Having friends is awesome," Zack says.

"But it's also a big responsibility. So take care of them."

"I will," Trey says, and Rhiannon snaps him away. Then she turns to the rest of us, her hands outstretched. Inside one of them is a teeny tiny crushed bug. Zack and the others lean over, looking at the little carcass. It's pretty gross. But something starts happening. Its skin is cracking like an egg, and something pops from underneath.

"Oliver-David," Rhiannon says, softly like her voice was a breath. "You're okay."

"Oliver-David," Zack says. "I barely recognize you."

This thing, this Oliver-David, looks like a bug. He's moving around Rhiannon's palm. He makes the sound of . . . well, he makes the sound of a fart, if I'm being honest. Little bits of sparkle dust rise up from his butt. It smells like a fart, too. I don't want to be rude, but I can't help but wave my hand in front of my face to ward off the smell.

"Of course I'm okay," Oliver-David says. "I just needed a little nap."

"Do you remember what happened?" Athena asks him.

"Sure I do. Bumblebee bats always remember their dreams. I was . . ." His voice trails off. "Well, it's none of your business, really."

"That's all right, Oliver-David," Rhiannon says.

"About that," the bug says. "I have an announcement to announce, a decision I've decided, a choice I've chosen."

"I'm all ears," Rhiannon says.

"I don't want to be Oliver-David anymore. I don't think I'm cut out for my name in lights after all. From now on you can call me by my given name."

"You got it, Melvin," Rhiannon says.

"Melvin," Zack says. "Really?"

"That's my name; don't wear it out!"

"Whatever you decide to call yourself,"

Rhiannon says, "I believe you are destined for greatness after all."

"Zack," I say. "My body is tingling again."

"Mine too," he says. "I think it's time to go home."

And so that's where we go.

Well, not home exactly. We go to Uncle Max's house. He's just getting back himself when we arrive. "I trust you had a better day today, Quinn," he says.

"Well," I start. "Not exactly. You see, first—"

"Hang on, Quinn," Zack says. "We're back on Earth time now, so we have to go to school. We can't be late. It's all about balance, right, Uncle Max?"

Uncle Max winks at him. "Right," he says.

"Cool," Zack says. "Because I'm excited to see Eli at school. He's got a new card trick to teach me."

"I'll be waiting for you both when you're done," Uncle Max says.